AN AMISH COUNTRY TREASURE 2

RUTH PRICE

Copyright © 2015 Ruth Price

All rights reserved.

ISBN:1517375959
ISBN-13:9781517375959

TABLE OF CONTENTS

ACKNOWLEDGMENTS	I
CHAPTER ONE	1
CHAPTER TWO	9
CHAPTER THREE	17
CHAPTER FOUR	25
CHAPTER FIVE	33
CHAPTER SIX	41
CHAPTER SEVEN	51
CHAPTER EIGHT	59
CHAPTER NINE	67
CHAPTER TEN	75
CHAPTER ELEVEN	81
CHAPTER TWELVE	89
CHAPTER THIRTEEN	95

CHAPTER FOURTEEN	103
CHAPTER FIFTEEN	111
CHAPTER SIXTEEN	121
CHAPTER SEVENTEEN	129
CHAPTER EIGHTEEN	137
CHAPTER NINETEEN	145
CHAPTER TWENTY	153
CHAPTER TWENTY-ONE	161
CHAPTER TWENTY-TWO	169
CHAPTER TWENTY-THREE	177
CHAPTER TWENTY-FOUR	183
CHAPTER TWENTY-FIVE	189
CHAPTER TWENTY-SIX	195
AN AMISH COUNTRY TREASURE 3	203
ABOUT THE AUTHOR	211

ACKNOWLEDGMENTS

All Praise first to the Almighty God who has given me this wonderful opportunity to share my words and stories with the world. Next, I have to thank my family, especially my husband Harold who supports me even when I am being extremely crabby. Further, I have to thank my wonderful friends and associates with Global Grafx Press who support me in every way as a writer. Lastly, I wouldn't be able to do any of this without you, my readers. I hold you in my heart and prayers and hope that you enjoy my books.

All the best and Blessings,

Ruth.

CHAPTER ONE

Jemima waited until night had fallen and the moon began its slow arc across the sky. When its smiling silver face appeared in the corner of her bedroom window, when the house had been quiet for hours, and when everyone else was asleep – she crept downstairs and out onto the front porch.

The moon was so bright that it cast shadows across the front yard, and the crickets hummed invisibly from the meadow.

Jemima sat down on the porch steps and looked out across the soft darkness, fragrant of mown grass and roses. She had always come to this spot as a child when she had been confused or upset because it was safe and quiet, and a good spot from which to watch the stars.

She looked up into the infinite night sky and questioned it with her eyes.

The George Washington letter was worth a million dollars

– that was what the experts had said. And she'd been sure that once she'd given it to him, Brad Williams, the Englischer reporter, would've grabbed the letter and run. She'd been sure that he'd have sold it and gotten rich and never bothered her again.

But he hadn't done that.

She was still in shock.

Instead – unbelievably – he had thrown it right back into her lap.

Jemima had a fleeting suspicion that his gesture might still be some clever reporter's trick, but what could he hope to gain by giving the letter back – and giving up a fortune?

She had been taught to be wary of the Englisch, but what could she say when the Englisch fellow could simply have taken the million dollars – and yet chose instead to give it back to her? Who would ever have guessed that an Englischer could pass up the chance to be rich?

A strange tingling danced down her neck. What if the Englisch reporter really did mean what he said about wanting to see her again – for her own sake?

She pressed her brow against her arms. But of course, that was impossible, and would be wrong, anyway. He wasn't Amish, and so they had nothing in common.

Her thoughts returned to the thick, official-looking letters from the appraisers. They were a secret that she'd tucked away in the little hidden space behind her bedroom wall. She had told no one about them, not even her mother.

The ghost of a smile played across her lips. No matter what else happened, she was glad that the love letter itself had turned out to be real. It had been so sweet – so much the words of a man in love. Who would have thought it?

She wondered briefly if Martha Washington had been as pierced by its beauty as she had been herself.

Wouldn't it be wonderful to have a husband who wrote you such letters?

She looked up at the sky, and just because there was no one there but her and God, and because there wasn't another soul awake within miles, she allowed herself to dream.

A tiny star trembled in the unfathomable distance and she watched it wistfully. If only there was a man who would tremble like that when she kissed him.

And who would tell her about his feelings so she didn't have to guess!

She closed her eyes. That was why the letter had been so beautiful. It had been written by a lover, not just a husband. A man who knew how to make himself vulnerable. A man who was strong enough to risk showing his heart without any attempt to protect it.

There were many boys who were willing to chase her, to kiss her, and do things for her. But not one of them, so far at least, had been willing to be naked in front of her – emotionally naked – and wasn't that what it truly meant to be intimate?

Wasn't love all about becoming vulnerable? Wasn't that…how you knew what it was?

That was what she dreamed of, at any rate: a man who was strong enough to let love make him vulnerable. Who would open his heart and share his feelings. And none of the boys who were chasing her had made the faintest attempt. Clearly, that was because they didn't know that was what she really wanted.

But if she told them, then they'd all say what she wanted to hear, and she'd never know if it had been real or not.

Jemima opened her eyes. She knew that Mark and Samuel and Joseph were all capable of making themselves vulnerable to her. Maybe they were just too busy competing with each other to notice that she was looking for a man who knew how to lose his heart.

Not win a contest.

She sighed.

But, of course, that was just wishful thinking. Her mother had told her many times that romance was not the same as happiness, and Jemima knew that she was right. A man's integrity – his devotion to God and to his family – was what really made him a good husband.

And that was what made it so hard to choose between Mark and Samuel and Joseph. They were all good, they all had integrity, they all loved God and they would all be good providers.

And since they were all equally good, and all of them would likely make good husbands – would it be sinful of her to hope that she could find one who would make a good lover, as well?

Her mouth turned down gently. Not one, so far, had even told her that he loved her.

She had no doubt that all of them did – but they were Amish boys, and had been raised to show rather than tell.

Mark especially. She knew that he would do anything on earth for her, but he wasn't one to talk about it. Her lips curved, as she remembered all the ways he had shown her that he loved her: he never let her carry anything, he gave her candy and bites of his lunch and little gifts he had made with his hands – a carved wooden box, a tiny bird made out of copper wire, and pressed flowers. But Mark felt deeply, she knew.

And Samuel – he was far more likely to kiss her, than to murmur sweet nothings in her ear. But sometimes he looked at her with so much love in his eyes that it wasn't really necessary to hear the words. They were all there – right on his face. And when he took her hand, his touch was so tender and gentle that she would have had to have been a fool not to know that he loved her.

Joseph Beiler had big, melting brown eyes and thick dark hair and was as handsome as any movie star. But he was so shy that he was hardly able to string two words together in front of her – poor Joseph! Then he tried to make up for it by writing her poetry. She made a face, remembering his last effort: he had compared her to a beautiful cow. Her sister Deborah had been rude, but right: Joseph's heart was pure, but he was a terrible lover.

She looked up at the stars wistfully. Just now and then, it would be so nice to have a boy tell her what he felt when he looked at her. To let her see inside his heart.

And it wouldn't hurt at all, if he did it well.

Jemima brushed a tendril of hair out of her eyes. Her mother had told her many times that it was foolish to have your head turned by flowery words and pretty gestures.

"A good man shows love by what he does, Jemima," had been her teaching. "Not by what he says."

Jemima frowned. Her mother's wisdom had seemed so clear and right just a few days ago, and she knew that it was the truth. But even so, she was confused.

Because by that reasoning, her childhood friends and

current suitors weren't the only ones who loved her. A strange Englisch reporter that she hardly knew had just shown her love.

Sort of.

And that made no sense at all.

CHAPTER TWO

Five o'clock came far too early the next morning, at least for Jemima King.

She dragged herself out of bed while it was still dark, dressed, and helped her mother cook breakfast; but she nodded over the stove as she cooked the eggs.

"Mind your hand, Jemima!" her mother cried sharply, and Jemima jerked her fingers back just in time to keep them from being burned on the hot metal. "Good heavens, child, you're sleepy! Didn't you get your rest?"

Jemima looked up at her apologetically. "No, I-I didn't get enough sleep last night," she confessed, blushing.

"Are you feeling all right?" her mother frowned, and put a hand to her cheek.

Jemima nodded, and the cloud lifted from her mother's brow. "Well, you must go to bed earlier tonight," she told her.

"Now help me set out breakfast. We can't be late for worship."

It was a Sunday morning, and worship was being held at the home of Aaron Kauffman, Samuel's father. It was on the far side of their church district, and it would therefore be necessary to get an early start.

Jemima set out a platter of sliced ham, and a bowl of biscuits, and fried potatoes. She was grateful when it came time to sit down, but she wondered how on earth she would ever stay awake through a two-hour sermon when she was starting out so tired.

Jacob King came walking in, stretching and yawning. "Good morning, my girls!" he told them, and leaned over to give their mother a peck on the cheek. "Ready for worship? It's a fine, fair morning, and not too hot. Are we set to eat?"

Rachel nodded, and sat down quickly. They all said a silent prayer, and then ate. Everyone but Jemima seemed to be in a good mood. Even Deborah wore a neutral expression through the meal, and for her that was as good as a smile.

But Jemima was worrying about the letter and chewed her thumbnail instead of her food. She could hardly concentrate on eating, wondering what on earth she was supposed to do now that she owned a document worth a million dollars. Nothing like that had ever happened to anyone she knew, or to anyone she had ever even heard about. What was she supposed to do now?

It felt sinful and greedy to keep such a thing. Surely such an important letter should be in a museum somewhere, not hidden away in a bank vault in her name.

But it would also feel sinful and greedy to sell it. A million dollars! What would an Amish girl like her even do with all that money? She already had all she needed, and it wasn't right to want more than that.

But, on the other hand, she had already tried to give it away, and to her total amazement that hadn't worked.

"Jemima!"

Jemima came to herself with a start. When she looked up, everyone at the table was staring at her.

"I-I'm sorry, I was-I was daydreaming," she stammered.

"About one of those silly pups, I suppose," her father replied, shaking his head. "Never mind, Mima! Just come along. It's time to get on the road."

Jemima followed them as they left. She climbed up into the buggy, and settled into the back seat, and watched the passing countryside without seeing it.

Maybe she should ask her parents what to do. But she dreaded the scolding they were sure to give her about talking to the Englisch reporter in the first place.

Then, too, if she told them what had happened, it would be

the end of her own choice in the matter: they would forbid her to talk to any Englischer, ever again, as long as she lived.

And she would never find out if the Englisch reporter had meant what he'd said – or not.

She nibbled off another corner of her nail.

When they arrived at the Kauffman's home, she drifted alongside her family, nodding in response to greetings and keeping her eyes on the ground.

But soon Samuel appeared at her elbow, looking love at her out of those beautiful blue eyes.

"I missed you," he smiled, and a tender look was on his face. "Is your family staying for lunch, Jemima?" he asked in a lower voice. "I was hoping you and I could talk somewhere privately afterwards."

She looked up at him, and was about to answer, when her father noticed them. "Good morning, Samuel!" he said loudly. He clapped Samuel on the shoulder, pushed right in between them, and smiled broadly. "Beautiful morning, isn't it?"

"Yes, sir," Samuel replied, much less enthusiastically.

"And so much friendliness, everywhere I turn!" he added, shaking Samuel's shoulder. Samuel looked up at him with a chagrined expression.

"Jemima, go and find your mother and sister a place to sit and hold it for them," her father commanded, and she nodded submissively. She shot Samuel an apologetic look over her shoulder, and was grateful to see that his eyes were still fastened to hers.

But when she looked back again, just before entering the Kauffman's barn, she saw with a sinking heart that her father was talking earnestly to Samuel, and that her handsome blond admirer looked as though he'd been rained on.

She found a nice empty spot at the end of a bench, and waited for her mother and sister.

And sighed.

Soon her mother and Deborah arrived and settled in beside her, and the benches began to fill up. Jemima noticed Samuel took a seat just across from them on the front row of the men's benches. His eyes were on hers, and she smiled at him faintly. His eyes sparkled, and he winked at her – just once. It was over like lightning, and she doubted that anyone else even saw it. She lowered her head, to hide her laughter, but when she looked up again, she noticed that her father's eyes were on her and she assumed a more pious expression.

The service started with the singing of hymns, and after they were over, the sermon. The minister opened his Bible and began talking.

Jemima felt herself beginning to zone out. She was sleepy, she was confused about the letter, and she was distracted by Samuel. Because now and then, when she looked up, he would catch her eye. And do something silly.

Like flick his tongue out over his lower lip, like a snake. And she would have to lower her head again and try not to laugh.

Or roll his eyes up toward the ceiling, as if he were about to pass out. That time, she had to bite her lip to keep from laughing.

But eventually her father noticed where she was looking and gave Samuel such a freezing look that he had to stop playing.

The preacher talked and talked, and to Jemima it seemed that the sermon would never end. But at some point, after she had gotten quiet and had settled down, the words that the preacher was saying started to reach her.

He was talking about being a good Christian, and how that meant being kind to the poor. Jemima sighed and crossed her legs and looked through a window at the beautiful summer afternoon outside. She had heard this many times before.

But suddenly he raised his Bible in the air, and said:

"What if a miracle happened? What if I suddenly had a million dollars and yet kept it all for myself? What kind of a Christian would let a neighbor stay hungry? Or cold, or sick, if he had the power to help him?"

Jemima gasped, and rolled stricken eyes to the man's face. He was looking right at her.

"It's the duty of a Christian to do as Jesus would do," the man said earnestly. "And Jesus fed the hungry, and took care of the sick."

Jemima's eyes filled with quick tears.

"If we follow Jesus, we must do those things, too."

Jemima felt herself going hot. She lowered her face, to hide the tears in her eyes.

The man's words had pierced her heart like a sharp arrow. It was like God had spoken through him, straight to her.

She had prayed to God, asking Him what she should do with the letter. And she hadn't heard any answer.

Until now.

Now it was crystal clear. This, this was her answer: she was to sell the letter, and give the money to people who needed it.

It answered everything. She would not be selfishly hiding the letter away; she would not be greedily spending the money on herself. The money could be used to feed her hungry neighbors, and help those who were sick and needed medical help.

And that would even explain why the Englischer had given the letter back to her against all reason: it had plainly been the will of God – a miracle.

She lifted her eyes to the ceiling and put her palms up, in a gesture of pure gratitude to God. She mouthed silent words of worship, and smiled to herself.

And when she opened them again, she noticed that Samuel Kauffman was staring at her face. The silly look was gone.

His eyes were dead serious now. And the look in them was that of a man who would run through fire.

CHAPTER THREE

After the service, there was always a light lunch served inside the house and outside on the lawn. Jemima, like all the other girls, helped serve her elders until it was her own turn to dine.

It was a fine, clear morning with a blue sky and green grass and white tablecloths and people talking and laughing. Many of Jemima's elders greeted her pleasantly as she brought plates or pitchers to their tables.

Most of the boys stole shy glances at her face. She dimpled, and smiled at them, and watched in amusement as their faces went pink.

Afterwards, she joined her family and listened in dutiful

silence as her father and their next-door neighbor talked crops. When she let her gaze wander, she noticed that Samuel was sitting at a table nearby. He was hard to miss when he took his hat off, his blond hair shone like corn silk against his black jacket. She noticed some of the other girls looking at him when he turned away, and she felt a little glow of gratitude. She was a lucky girl to have such a handsome young man pursuing her.

And he was pursuing her. It didn't take him long to sense her eyes on him. He smiled, and then got serious again and looked at her with such frank intent that she felt herself going hot. Samuel had beautiful blue eyes, and they expressed every feeling going through his heart as clearly as any sign.

She looked at him through her lashes. That was Samuel's charm – his glib laughter, and his carelessness, was all an act. He couldn't hide his true feelings – his eyes betrayed him every time.

And what his eyes were saying to her at the moment was probably best not said in a room full of people.

Jemima smiled faintly, well pleased, and dropped her own gaze demurely.

After everyone had eaten lunch, and she was free, Samuel appeared at her elbow. He whisked her away with him so quickly that even her father – who was talking to a neighbor about horseshoes – didn't have time to see them go.

Samuel took her hand and led her down a tortuous path that twisted crazily through a side door, down a few steps, through a narrow doorway, up a few stairs, and into a small sitting room in a hidden corner of their house.

Then he closed the door behind them and pulled her into his arms without another word.

Jemima went into them without a murmur and turned her face up to be kissed.

Samuel pulled her to his chest, twined his strong fingers in hers, pressed both hands behind her back, and kissed her with delicious tenderness. He was a delightful kisser – his lips seemed made for light, playful caresses, and he would pause mid-pucker sometimes, to pull back and look down at her until she opened her eyes. Then he would go on quirky kissing tangents, one kiss on each of her closed eyelids, lots of little kisses along her brows, and he might even plant a few stray kisses in the delicate, sensitive spot under her ear.

She giggled suddenly, and shook her head. "Oh, Samuel, that tickles," she laughed, turning her face away teasingly. "Didn't you shave your chin this morning?"

He looked down at her with a smile, and rubbed it with one brown hand. "Now that you mention it," he admitted ruefully, and his smile widened to a grin. "Tell me, does the scruffy look do anything for me?" He turned his profile, and she giggled again.

Then the smile faded from his lips. A serious look replaced them,

He pulled back, taking both her hands in his. "Jemima, I brought you here because I wanted to talk to you alone. I have something to say to you."

She held his gaze, waiting.

An uncharacteristic wave of shyness seemed to overwhelm him. "We-we've known each other a long time," he stammered.

"Yes, Samuel." She smiled, remembering the first time she had seen Samuel: he had been a mischievous little five-year-old boy making mud pies. He had looked up at her suddenly, his blue eyes and blond hair in stark contrast to a face covered in black mud. She had screamed and run away, and he had chased her.

He seemed to read the thought off her face. He relaxed a bit, and chuckled. "Yes, we go way back, don't we, Mima?" he said softly.

She looked up into his eyes and nodded, giving him her earnest attention.

"You know what kind of person I am, and I hope you feel about me, the same way I feel about you."

He massaged her hand gently, and half-smiled.

"After all – I asked to court with you, and you agreed."

Jemima's heartbeat quickened. She leaned in and looked deep into his beautiful eyes. Maybe Samuel was finally going to show her his heart. He might even tell her that he loved her.

And since he seemed to be shy, maybe she could help things along and give him a little nudge. Maybe she could gently remind him that there were other boys who might be willing to admit they loved her.

Maybe then he would confess his love, and pour out his heart, and make himself vulnerable – like in that magical letter.

She took a deep breath. "Yes, Samuel, we have been good friends. I agreed to see you. Not to see just you, but to go out. Just like you can see other girls, and not just me."

He raised his eyes to hers, and the look in them now was determined. Jemima's pulse quickened in anticipation. He was going to tell her he loved her at last. He was going to say it.

"I don't want to go out with any other girls, Jemima. And I don't want you to go out with any other men."

She held his eyes. "Why not, Samuel?" she asked gently.

Samuel looked pained. "Jemima, I-I–"

There was suddenly a thunder of pounding feet outside, and two little girls burst into the room, laughing and giggling.

"Abby, you're it!" shrieked a little pigtailed girl. "I caught you!"

"Count to ten!" the other one cried, and pressed herself against the wall. "One two three four…"

The pigtailed girl streaked out into the hall, only to collide with her outraged mother. "Ruth Beiler, stop that this instant! The noise you make – this isn't our house!"

She looked in and caught sight of the other child. "Abby Stoltzfus, is that you? Come out now, and stop this nonsense!"

The child obeyed in subdued silence, and the woman finally noticed Jemima and Samuel standing there. She looked embarrassed.

"Oh – I'm sorry," she murmured, and hustled the children out, but not before casting another curious, and frankly speculative glance at them.

After the door had closed behind the intruders, Samuel ran a hand through his rumpled blond hair, looked up at the ceiling, and then down at Jemima with a rueful sigh.

Jemima could have cried in frustration. There had been a confession trembling on Samuel's very lips, and it was slipping away – she could feel it. She pressed her hands against his chest.

"Oh Samuel, never mind them," she said earnestly, "you

were going to tell me something. Don't hold back – I'm listening! Tell me now."

He smiled, gave a self-deprecating shrug, and cupped her cheek with his hand. "Mima," he said tenderly, "I–"

He leaned close. Jemima searched his eyes with her own, but to her disappointment, no tender confession followed.

Unless she counted the gentle, softly rhythmic kiss that communicated so much.

And admitted exactly nothing.

CHAPTER FOUR

A week passed, in which Samuel called at the house again and used his handsome lips to kiss her much and confess little; Mark called at the house also, and also kissed her much, and told her even less; and Joseph mailed three regrettable pages of poetry in which he compared her to a large chicken, though she was fairly sure he was trying to say that she would make a good wife, in a very roundabout way.

She hadn't had much time to think about the letter, but the memory of it nagged at her. She had received what she believed to be direction from God to sell it, and the proper thing to do now was to call that Englisch reporter and get it over with.

But she dreaded it.

She counted it sheer Divine Intervention that he hadn't kept the letter for himself. That must surely be it, because she had no confidence in the fellow's ethics, or, to be honest, his sanity. He'd behaved like a madman the first day she met him. And his behavior hadn't improved – the last time she'd seen him, he'd jumped at her from the bushes in her mother's garden, like a wild animal.

He even pretended to be interested in her, though they were total strangers.

Still, it was her duty to sell the letter, and she supposed she'd better get on with it and have done. And since the crazy Englischer was the only person she knew that could help her, she guessed she ought to call him up.

Of course, it would all be very awkward, and not at all proper. As an Amish woman, she was not supposed to talk to Englischers and Englisch men in particular. But in a case like this, what other choice did she have?

She couldn't think of any other choice, anyway. But once the letter had been sold, and she had the money, no one would have to know what she'd done. She would just be an anonymous donor to people who needed help.

There was one possible problem, though: the Englisch reporter had said he wanted to write a story about her. That part did worry her. But since she didn't intend to see him again if she could help it, she supposed it would be all right to tell him her story over the phone.

There was little danger that her family and friends would ever find out. No one she knew read Englisch papers or visited their websites.

She sat on the porch swing, shelling beans into a big metal bowl. She still had the little card the reporter had given her. She could go out to the little phone shack at the end of their driveway and call. She would tell the Williams fellow to go ahead and put the letter up for auction.

Maybe she wouldn't even have to see him again at all. Maybe she could just tell him to take pictures of the letter, and tell him her story over the phone and tell him not to share her name.

Yes, that was it! She would give him permission to tell the story but not use her name. Then no one, not even the people who read the story, would ever know it was her.

Yes, that would be perfect. She smiled to herself, comforted by the belief that even if she had to do some unusual things at first, everything would be all right in the end.

Jemima put her plan into action early the next day.

At sunrise, she sat patiently on a small bench in the phone

shack. The phone rang and rang…four times, five, six.

She wondered why the Englischer didn't answer his phone. He had written that he was staying at the motel outside of town. Surely he was up by now – it was almost 6 a.m., and the sky had been light for almost an hour.

After the tenth ring, there was a fumbling sound, and a clunk, and more fumbling. A bleary, irritable voice snapped:

"Very funny, Delores! Six o'clock in the morning! I'm reporting you to Dapper Dwayne for employee abuse. He'll be sending you a list of my grievances."

Jemima frowned. "I must have the wrong number," she stammered, and prepared to hang up the phone.

There was a frantic fumbling sound on the other end, followed by: "No, no, um, yes, this is Brad Williams. I'm sorry – is this – is this Miss Jemima King?"

Jemima frowned. He was babbling like a lunatic, and she was seized by the urge to hang up the phone and forget the whole thing. But the remembrance of the sermon she had heard spurred her to take a new grip on her resolve.

She took a deep breath. "Yes, it is."

"Ah! Ah, I apologize, Miss King. I, ah, mistook you for someone else."

She set her mouth, and replied firmly: "I'm giving you permission to sell the letter for me. You can give it to those people, and they can put it up for auction."

"Wonderful! I'd be delighted to help you! Would you be open to meeting me in town and letting me drive you out to the auction house?"

Jemima frowned into the receiver. His voice sounded absurdly excited. She shook her head, thinking: Greed.

"I'm not going to meet with anybody," she told him firmly, "and I'm not going to the auction house, and I'm not going to get my picture taken. But if you want to ask me questions, I'll tell you about how I found the letter. But only if you don't use my name or my family's name."

"Ah." There was a split-second of silence, followed by: "I ah, appreciate that, Miss King! I would absolutely like to ask you questions about how you found the letter! Maybe I could come out to your house, it would only be for a—"

She shook her head vehemently. "No, I don't want anyone to come out to my house!"

"Okay, I understand," he replied quickly. "We can do it over the phone! I'll call you the day before the sale – when everything is ready."

"I'll call you," she told him.

"Or, you could call me," he amended quickly.

Jemima looked out the window toward the house. She only

had a few minutes.

When she returned to the conversation, the reporter was saying, "Call me at this same number next Monday, about noon. I'll walk you through the small print, because there are some legal formalities. In order for us to sell the letter, you'll have to fill out some forms, and give the auction house your written permission to sell."

Jemima frowned. "Will they keep my name a secret?"

"If you want that."

Jemima nodded. "I do."

"I, ah, the appraisers recommended Brinkley's, is that all right with you?"

"Who's Brinkley?"

There was a long silence. "Ah…I'm sorry…Brinkley's is the auction house."

"As long as they keep my name private, and don't come out to the house or bother my family, I don't care who sells it," Jemima answered.

She looked up and saw her father standing on the front lawn with his hands on his hips. He was looking for her. Rufus was hitched to the buggy, and it was time to go back to Mr. Satterwhite's with the batch of dolls that she'd promised him.

"I have to go," she said suddenly. "I have to go to town."

"Wait – I mean, is it all right if I mail the documents to your home? You'll have to–"

But Jemima was no longer paying attention. Her father had stumped off to the garden, and she knew that once he missed her there, he'd be coming in the direction of the phone shack.

And she couldn't afford to be caught in it.

She dropped the phone and decamped, hoping that she could reach the lawn before her father returned.

Meanwhile, the phone receiver swung back and forth, as the reporter's tiny, agitated voice spooled out uselessly into the air.

CHAPTER FIVE

Delores Watkins nursed a large cup of steaming black coffee between two large, brightly-manicured hands. The rays of the rising sun dawned through the office window behind her. They tinged the back of her large brown bouffant hairdo like an orange halo, and glimmered off the backs of her earrings.

A green box suddenly appeared on her computer screen. She cursed softly and fluently, put her coffee cup down, and gingerly placed a headset on her carefully-coiffed hair.

"Hello?"

Brad William's voice was already running, non-stop, on the other end. She rolled her eyes up toward the ceiling.

"Stop. Stop, Brad. It's too early. What? No, slow down."

She lifted the cup and took another sip, frowning.

"So, she did call you. Congratulations."

"You promised her you'd do what? Now wait a minute. Yes, it's good; it has the potential to be – yes, yes. But you represent the Ledger. I can't just let you go running off to the most prestigious auction house in the country without–"

She took another sip.

"Yes, I was implying that. And posturing will get you nowhere.

"I never said no. But we're going to have to talk to Dapper Dwayne and do a little legal CYA before I'll even think about letting you call the auction house.

"I don't care.

"Cry me an ocean, Brad.

"Okay, you're lucky that I don't can you for that. Remember that there are plenty of other guys who'd be glad to --

The little box disappeared from the screen, and Delores rolled her eyes and removed the headset. Her assistant entered the room just then, saw her face, and looked at her quizzically. She shrugged and smiled.

"It was Brad on the phone," she explained.

The young woman grinned, and put a folder on her desk. "Oh. What is it this time?"

Delores took another pull from the coffee cup. "Oh, nothing.

"The kid may have the biggest story of the year – that's all."

Back at Uncle Bob's Amish Motel, Brad Williams was coming to much the same conclusion.

He sat on the edge of the motel bed, wearing nothing but a pair of boxer shorts. He held his head in his hands, and his mind was racing.

Delores was infuriating, but upon mature reflection, he had to admit that she was right to be cautious.

Because he couldn't be.

He had the mother of all feature stories. All he had to do was reel it in. Once they'd cleared the legal stuff with Dapper Dwayne – and he was convinced it was just a formality – he was going to have a hand in one of the biggest and most historic auction sales in American history.

The story was sure to go viral, especially if he could get that girl to change her mind about the picture. She was just made for the camera.

He allowed himself to picture it. That gorgeous face would sell the story instantly on social media. Every man in America would be seeing that face in his dreams, and every woman would be trying to recreate it with makeup – in vain.

He closed his eyes and conjured it up in his mind: the tiny curls just below the little cap, the smooth, placid brow, the light, perfectly arched brows. The huge green eyes, so effortlessly seductive in their beautiful innocence. The delicate nose and the plump, pouting lips that have haunted him since they'd first met. What would it feel like to be kissed by those lips?

He shook his head slightly, and forced himself to focus.

Of course, there was one big hitch. He'd promised not to take a photo of her face. He still had no idea why he'd promised her that. Probably, it was because she turned him into a babbling idiot.

He fumbled over the nightstand for a cigarette. He lit one, inhaled deeply, and stretched back out on the bed.

It must've been the thought of her lips on the other end of the line. Or that voice. He closed his eyes, remembering it. Her voice was smooth, and soft, and so gentle and feminine that it distracted him from what she'd actually been saying.

No, mostly he remembered – no names, no pictures, no appearance at the auction house, and no visits to her home from anyone else.

He took another drag from the cigarette.

Of course, he couldn't keep all those the promises he'd made to her. He felt a flicker of guilt about it, but he couldn't. He might as well just give up on the story, and he'd stuck his neck out way too far for that. He'd given up too much for that.

When he'd opened Jemima's letter, and a 200-year-old document, signed by George Washington had fallen out on the motel bed, it had taken every last atom of will power for him not to take it and cash in. He still didn't understand completely why he hadn't. It would've been technically ethical to accept – she had given it to him, after all.

But somehow, he couldn't. It was as simple as that.

Maybe it was the idea of taking money from a woman. And not just any woman – a young, gorgeous woman that, he had to admit, he wanted to impress.

Maybe it was ethics. Maybe he didn't want to think of himself as a creep or an opportunist. Maybe he wanted to make his own money.

Or maybe he just liked doing things the hard way. It was the story of his life, after all. It was why he was going to die poor, and probably young.

Delores' disgusted face popped into his mind, and he sputtered smoke as he tamped the cigarette out. Another of his bad habits.

And he had plenty. What was more, he was tired of being a good boy. He had just ruined himself and turned down a fortune, out of some quixotic idea of being his own man. Well, now that he was guaranteed rocky sledding for the rest of his life, he might as well steer the sled himself.

It was time to return to the real world.

He couldn't stay away from Jemima, not if he wanted the story. That decision was as simple as his decision not to take the money. He'd be risking everything, but without Jemima's picture, the story was going nowhere anyway.

Somehow, he had to get her to let him take a photo, and it wasn't going to be easy. It was against her religion, for one thing. She didn't know him, for another. He got the definite feeling that she didn't trust him and, possibly, that she might even be frightened of him.

Of course, that was because he hadn't exactly been Mr. Smooth so far. He had done everything wrong when it came to gaining her trust.

And that was a first.

He frowned at the ceiling. He didn't like to admit it, but that gorgeous redhead threw him right off his game. His decision to hide in the bushes at her house definitely hadn't been well thought out.

Which brought him to his reason for that choice: her volcano of a father. Her very mountainous, very fiery, very rumbling old man.

If the red giant caught him anywhere near Jemima…? Brad closed his eyes, and had a sudden vision of himself flying through the air and landing ingloriously, and in great confusion, on his rearward parts.

He had to get Jemima away from her father, and preferably from everybody else as well. And once he did – well, she'd laid down a lot of conditions over the phone, but he was confident that he'd be able to change all that, if he could just get alone with her.

At least, that was how it usually worked – when he applied himself.

He sprang out of bed and made for the shower.

CHAPTER SIX

Brad parked the company truck in a parking space as far away from the Satterwhite Gift Shop as he could manage. He didn't want to advertise his presence.

There was no sign of a buggy outside the shop, and he had no guarantee that Jemima would be there. But she had mentioned going to town, and if she supplied merchandise to that cantankerous old man, it was at least possible that today was the day.

He climbed out of the truck and scanned the street. There was no sign of her, but, he smiled suddenly, it looked like the store had a back door. He ducked into a cramped alleyway between the old buildings, and weaved his way to the street behind.

He came out on the backside of the building, amidst dumpsters and unpainted wooden steps and loading docks – the side of the business that customers weren't meant to see.

He cracked a delighted grin. He'd been right. Sure enough, there was an Amish buggy. And better yet, it was empty.

He weaved through the boxes and trashcans, rehearsing the speech he had made up in his head on the way over.

I'm sorry Jemima, but I had to talk to you again. I need some information before I can go to the auction house, and I didn't get a chance to ask you.

Yeah, that might work, especially if she felt a little guilty about hanging up on him. It might at least keep her from running away.

Then he would add: *I can only help you if you work with me. I'll do all I can for you, but I can't do everything by myself.*

Then, he thought, he might give her a soulful look. He was aware that he had nice eyes – or at least, he'd been told so by enough women that he considered it probable.

After he'd given her the old puppy dog look, he could say: *Please, can you compromise just a little? Just a tiny photo, only one, for the article?*

No, that was too direct. He'd have to lead up to that.

Maybe he could go with: *Would you be willing to let me come out to the house again, very briefly, so we could talk face to face? Would you–*

A clattering sound from the back door of the shop made him duck behind a stack of crates. He stood there, with his heart pounding.

The old storekeeper's bald head appeared in the doorway. He was sweeping dust out of the storeroom, and a choking cloud filled the air. Brad turned his face away as it descended on him.

The old man turned and addressed someone inside the store. "It's a shame. You can't turn around these days without being pestered by strangers. I wish things could go back to the way they were, before tourism ruined everything."

A big, booming voice answered from inside the storeroom, and Brad flattened himself against the back wall of the store.

"Yes, it's true," the voice growled. "I wish – but it doesn't matter what I wish, because wishing won't make it so. We can only go about our own business, and hope that other people do the same." Jacob King's enormous shadow fell across the back doorway. "I'll be back in a few minutes, Eli," he told the old man. "Tell Jemima to wait here for me." He strode out onto the loading dock, and the wooden boards groaned under his feet.

The storekeeper followed as Jacob King climbed up into

the buggy. "Tell Jed I need some baling wire when you see him," he called.

Jacob King raised his hand in farewell, and the buggy clattered off down the back street. The storekeeper turned and went back inside immediately.

Brad stayed in hiding until he was sure the old man was gone, and then followed cautiously.

He leaped easily onto the small loading dock, and peered around the edge of the doorway. The small storeroom was empty, and the door to the sales floor was standing open.

He could see the old man through the doorway. His back was turned; he was standing at the cash register. Jemima was facing him, her lovely eyes turned to the old man's.

"Your Poppa wants you to wait for him here," the old man said kindly. "Why don't you take a bottle of pop from the fridge in the back?"

Jemima smiled at him, and the sight of her face made something in Brad's chest turn over. Every detail froze in his memory: the little wisps of coppery hair floating around her face. The way the light from the front window cupped the curve of her right cheek; how smooth and soft it looked. Her eyes. Those luminous, innocent eyes that never failed to make him think very guilty thoughts. He cursed under his breath, but it was useless; she had the face of an angel, and even that black outfit she was wearing couldn't hide the fact that that she had the body of one, as well.

The light behind her just outlined the delicate curve of a breast, smoothed in to the tiny waist, and curved out again over the hip, like a caress. He'd never felt it before, but suddenly he realized that it was possible to be more stirred by imagination than stark nakedness. To Brad's horror, his body abruptly put him on notice – it hadn't signed off on his plan to play it cool.

He rolled his head against the wall and closed his eyes, trying to remember his speech. After a few seconds it came back to him – and not an instant too soon. The sound of an approaching footfall in the doorway made his eyes fly open.

Jemima's startled gaze took him in as he crouched against the back wall. He straightened instantly. What was his opening line?

He opened his mouth to say: *I'm sorry Jemima, but I had to talk to you again.*

But what came out, with a croak, was: "I'm sorry, Jemima!"

He seized her shoulders, crushed her to him, and dug his face into hers. Then he kissed her more crazily than he'd ever kissed any woman in his life.

Her lips were as silky, as full, and as yielding as he had

dreamed. They melted against his like sugar dissolving on his tongue.

She froze in his arms. Her small hands curled up against his chest, and he could feel her sharp intake of breath.

Her body was as light as a feather against his, soft and tiny and beautifully fragile. He could feel her heart fluttering against his chest, like a snared bird trying to escape. His own was pounding like a hammer.

He was ruined, his life was over, and she'd hate him and take him for a lunatic stalker and a moron. Not only that, but he was going to be fired and he'd thrown away a million dollars and the story of a lifetime.

But oh, Duchess – it was all worth it!

And just for an instant, he could've sworn that something sparked between them. For a split-second, those heavenly lips moved.

Just before she clawed out of his arms.

"Oh, let go of me!" she hissed, but to his intense gratitude, she didn't scream. "Crazy Englischer–" she broke off into a long string of angry German-sounding words that really needed no translation.

Her almond-shaped eyes blazed. "I know what you were thinking, you – you Englischer reporter!" she spat, as if she could think of nothing worse. Her voice was low, but she was as angry as it was possible for a gentle girl to be.

"You want me to give you a big story, and you think that you can just kiss the simple Amish girl and make her do anything you say! Well, I've kissed plenty of boys before, and better boys than you, and they ask first, and kiss second!"

She jabbed a forefinger at his chest for emphasis: "And only if I say yes!"

Brad blinked at her. His face went hot. "You're totally right. I'm sorry, I shouldn't have done that," he stammered. He regained enough of his self-possession to attempt a pleading look, only to be captured by her eyes – again.

"It's true that I came here to talk to you about the story, but I-I forgot myself." He ran a hand through his hair in distraction. "I'm not like this, really. I'm a professional. It's just that you're – you really are the most beautiful girl I've ever met in my life."

The look in her eyes slowly changed. The anger swirling in them faded to puzzlement, and then to something that looked almost like–

He shook his head. "I am so sorry. There was no excuse for the way I behaved. I'll go away now and leave you alone." He glanced back over his shoulder, and bit his lip.

"I hope you don't let the – the way I acted keep you from selling the letter, though. I'll mail you the forms. Because I hope you get all the – the good things from it that you deserve. Here" – he scrabbled in his shirt pocket for a card – "here's the number of the auction house. You really shouldn't miss that auction, you know. It's a once-in-a-lifetime thing."

She reluctantly took the card from his hand, and he gave her a sickly smile.

Annnd it was time to leave.

He started out the back door, only to be confronted by the sound of the returning buggy. He blanched. It was her father.

He was a dead man.

Something touched his shoulder. When he looked down, it was her hand.

"I'll go out to him," the soft voice was saying. "Stay here until we're gone." She looked at him again, shook her head, and brushed past him.

He withdrew into the shadows, and watched as the buggy stopped, Jemima stepped up lightly, and the vehicle clattered away.

He couldn't help watching it as it went, and to his surprise, Jemima turned to look back at him just before it rolled out of sight.

He exhaled and collapsed against the wall. His heart was pounding out of his chest, electrified by a combined near-love and near-death experience. He slumped there, weak and trembling, for a full ten minutes.

But after his pulse had calmed down – a long while later – when he'd had a chance to think, maybe he wasn't ruined after all. Sure, he'd been a thumping moron, he'd lost his mind, and he'd gone way, way off script. He'd risked the story of a lifetime and his whole career. But–

Jemima hadn't screamed when he kissed her.

She hadn't handed him over to her father, when that would've been easy.

Of course, there was no way to know what that meant – if it meant anything.

Except, maybe, mercy. The Amish were big on mercy.

He closed his eyes in despair. But Delores Watkins was not big. At least, not big on mercy. He put his head in his hands and groaned.

CHAPTER SEVEN

Jacob King cast a quizzical look at his daughter as they drove out of town and into the countryside.

"What's the matter with you, Mima? Aren't you feeling well?"

Jemima rolled startled eyes to her father's worried ones. "I feel fine," she stammered.

He gave her a shrewd look, and chucked her under the chin with one big knuckle. "You look almost feverish. Your cheeks are flushed, your cap is off center, your hair is mussed and you look as if you'd seen a ghost. If I didn't know for sure that those boys of yours were at work right now, I'd say you were suffering from a bad case of puppy."

She gasped, and turned her eyes down to her lap.

But her father only laughed. "I suppose your Mamm is right. I am too hard on you – my poor girl! I guess I do see a puppy under every bush. But it's only because, so far, there has been one under there. Every time!"

He looked at her, laughed again, and turned his eyes back to the road. "It's what I get for having such a beautiful daughter."

Jemima looked up at him, but he was gazing out over the road. "Don't let your mother know I told you that," he said, without turning his head. "She'll say I'm teaching you to be vain."

Jemima smiled just a tiny bit, and reached for his hand. "Thank you, Daed," she said gratefully.

By the time they got home, it was midmorning, and the day promised to be fair and hot. Her father unhitched Rufus and took him back to the barn, and Jemima went inside the house.

Her mother was heavily embroiled in a major baking project. She was bending over the kitchen table with her hair flying from under her cap and flour up to her elbows. She was rolling out dough with a wooden pin. She looked up and cried out in relief.

"Oh, Jemima, there you are! How I missed you this morning! You would have been willing to help me, but your sister ran away, and I haven't seen her since breakfast. Just wait until I see her again – I haven't spanked her for years, but that's about to change!"

She raised one arm and wiped perspiration off her brow. "Help me with the chores, Jemima. I have fifteen pies to finish before the bake sale tomorrow, and I don't have time to do anything else. Go out and gather the eggs, and get a basket of greens for tonight, and when you finish that I need you to make lunch." She paused and closed her eyes. "Oh! Why I ever agreed to do so many baked goods, all at once, I don't know! It sounded like such a good idea at the time!"

Jemima leaned in and kissed her mother's cheek. "It still is," she told her. "I'll wash up and start right away."

"Hurry," her mother sighed.

Jemima ran quickly up the stairs, ducked into the bathroom, and gave herself a quick cat bath in front of the bathroom mirror.

But when she met her own eyes in the glass, she gasped to see the girl staring back at her. Her father had been right: she looked a mess. Her cap was all crooked, and her hair was all over, her eyes looked wild and she was flushed. She put one palm to her cheek, to cool it.

She lowered her head and pinched her lips together

angrily, and washed her hands a little too vigorously.

Then she walked into her own bedroom and closed the door behind her. She dug out the money that Mr. Satterwhite had given her for the dolls and tucked it away in the little hidden panel in the wall.

She frowned. There were the official-looking letters from the auction house, just where she had left them. But the whole thing was trouble, and the sooner she could sell the George Washington letter and have done with it, the better she'd like it!

She took the little panel in her hand, but as she moved to fasten it, another piece of paper came fluttering out onto the floor.

She bent down to pick it up. It was the business card the crazy Englischer had given to her. Her eyes darkened, and on an angry impulse, she pinched the little card between her fingers and tore it right in two.

That gave her a certain pleasure, but then the thought occurred to her: she couldn't just throw the pieces away, because if someone found them, how would she explain them?

Jemima pushed her lip into a pout that would have driven her admirers to frenzy had they seen it, and reluctantly pushed the torn pieces in with the other papers. She could hide them there, until she could safely destroy them.

She replaced the panel with a bit more force than was required, and turned her lips down in distress.

Crazy Englisch reporter – the very idea!

"Jemima!"

Her mother's voice floated up from downstairs, and Jemima took a deep breath, and shook her skirts out briskly, as if shaking off a distasteful memory. Then she hurried downstairs, and put the thought of the morning's shocking events from her mind.

Or, at least, she tried to put them from her mind. She found, to her dismay, that it was easier said than done. Confusion swirled in her brain, making it impossible to concentrate on her work.

She collected a few eggs in the hen house, but soon had to stop. The bewildered prayer welling up in her had to come out.

Why, God?

Jemima closed her eyes and pressed her brow against one of the hens. It was downy and warm, but it gave her no answer.

Why did this happen? Didn't You tell me to sell the letter? Wasn't Your message as clear as day? And weren't You the one making the Englischer help me?

But if that's true, then why did this happen? It ruins everything!

She opened her eyes, but she wasn't seeing the dim interior of the hen house. She was seeing a pair of bright blue eyes, glowing like electricity. Insane eyes.

Lord, what can I do? The wicked Englischer is the only person I know who can help me sell the letter. What now?

The soft muttering of the hens gave her no clue as to the answer. She shook her head.

When she had finished gathering eggs, she went and knelt in the garden on her hands and knees, and picked cherry tomatoes and carrots. Every now and then she looked over her shoulder and out into the bushes at the edge of the yard.

And imagined that she saw a branch move.

Then grumbled under her breath, and returned to work.

Jemima yanked a carrot out of the ground. The more she thought about the Englischer, the angrier she got. She had never been so shocked in all her life, or so outraged. Some people thought that they were so big and important, or maybe so handsome, that they could treat other people any way they liked.

But they were wrong.

She leaned back on her heels and swiped the dirt off of her hands.

Some people were so full of hochmut and – her eye fell on a wheelbarrow – *fertilizer* that they didn't care about other people's feelings, or rights.

Only their own.

She muttered under her breath and shook her head angrily. Her father had been right, the Englisch were crazy and greedy and you couldn't trust them when you were looking right at them, much less when your back was turned.

Her face went red, as that horrifying scenario flashed through her mind, and she yanked out another carrot.

CHAPTER EIGHT

The next morning was a perfect day for the bake sale: sunny, bright, and not too hot. At nine o'clock, Jemima was helping her mother set up a table at a neighborhood plant nursery. The owner had agreed to let their congregation hold the sale outside his shop.

Summer weekends were always good sale days, since those were the days that both locals and tourists came to the nursery to buy big, beautiful Amish garden plants.

And Amish-produced confections.

The congregation was holding the bake sale to raise money for little Adam Yoder who had fallen down a well and had broken a half-dozen bones. He had been in the hospital for days, and his medical bill was, reportedly, astronomical.

Jemima carried a sheet cake to the table and set it carefully between a basket of yeast rolls and a plate of blueberry muffins. Her mother had worked all day yesterday, and lots of other people from their congregation had as well.

But Jemima was depressed. She gazed out over the groaning tables and couldn't help thinking that it was a wasted effort. Even if the bake sale was a huge success, it could hardly raise the money that Adam's parents needed.

She thought of the letter gathering dust in the bank vault, and was pierced by guilt. The proceeds of that letter would be more than enough to relive Adam's parents of that crushing debt, and maybe, the debts of a lot more sick people, besides.

And here she stood, with all their neighbors, selling cakes that would bring ten dollars, at the most.

Jemima scanned the sale tables sadly. They had set them up outside the store, and those tables were now laden with every kind of temptation imaginable: her mother's mouth-watering blackberry pies and peach cobblers, friendship bread still warm from the oven, sticky buns, sugar cookies, and all manner of cakes. Some local farm families that made their own cheeses and hams were also selling their wares.

Including Mark's.

Jemima's expression lightened at the sight of him. Mark

was a welcome distraction from her guilt and her confusion. It was a comfort to see him. He was as strong and reliable as her father's watch.

He was already there, helping some of the other vendors unload their heavier boxes, since he was young and strong and – and muscular.

Jemima allowed herself the pleasure of watching him – discreetly – as he worked. Samuel was taller, and Joseph was more handsome, but Mark was by far the most well-built of her suitors. His arms were strong, his chest was broad, his hips were narrow, and his stomach was so flat that it actually curved in slightly.

He was almost a man now; he certainly didn't look much like her old childhood tormentor. But an old longing surged up inside her suddenly as she watched him – she longed to talk to Mark, like she had when they were children. She longed to get him alone and pour out her heart to him.

Mark didn't talk much, but he was a wonderful listener. She knew he would never betray her, not to anyone.

Of course she couldn't tell him about the letter, or the crazy Englischer, but – maybe she could just ask him what he would do – if something unexpected and – and difficult happened.

Mark had always been so practical and down to earth. He had so much common sense – and after the craziness of the last few weeks, she yearned for that.

Jemima looked around for her mother, and to her relief, she was facing in the other direction talking to some of the other women.

Jemima backed away from the table, and disappeared into the nursery, shielding herself behind racks of seedlings and big potted trees. She peered out, looking for Mark. He was unloading boxes about ten feet away.

She moved closer, still keeping herself out of sight, and when he passed close by, she called softly from behind a ficus bush.

"Mark!"

He stopped, and looked around in puzzlement.

"Mark, here!"

He stepped closer, frowning slightly. "Mima? What are you doing hiding in the bushes?"

Jemima felt her face going red, but she was committed now, and she had to follow through. She looked up at him pleadingly.

"I-I wanted to talk to you. Alone, someplace. Away from all these people," she begged. "Can you get away – just for a few minutes?"

He looked at her eyes, and his expression softened. "Of

course," he said, and put the box down on a table nearby. "Where do you want to go?"

Jemima was embarrassed to feel tears pool in her eyes. "Oh, anywhere," she told him, "just away from everybody. Just somewhere we can be alone!"

He looked at her again. "Okay." He put a hand lightly under her elbow, and guided her out through to the farthest edge of the nursery. He led her to a little nook, mostly hidden behind a row of potted evergreens, and they sat down together in a garden swing.

He looked into her eyes with a concerned expression. "What's the matter, Mima? Has something upset you?"

Jemima felt her lip trembling, and she looked away, irritated by her own weakness. She shook her head, and strove to control her voice. "It's just – something strange has happened, Mark," she said, keeping her eyes on a nearby tree. "Something very strange. And I don't know what to do."

She turned her eyes back to his, and looked into them pleadingly. "And I thought, maybe, you could give me some advice."

Mark took her hands in his and nodded. "Of course, Mima. You know that. Anything."

Jemima looked up at him. "Mark, I-I have a decision to make. A very important decision. I think, I believe, that I have guidance from God about what to do. But something just happened that – that has confused me, very much, and I-I'm not so sure anymore."

He was watching her intently, but at this, his eyes burned. "Has someone…has someone done something they shouldn't, Jemima?" he asked.

Jemima felt a wave of fire roll over her cheeks. Mark clenched his jaw, nodded angrily, looked up at the sky, and then back at her.

"I think I know what I should do, Mark," she whispered, looking up into his eyes, "but now I'm – I'm scared."

Mark was frowning now, and looked angry. "No one's hurt you, have they, Mima?" he demanded. "Or threatened you? Because if they have–"

Jemima shook her head. "Oh, no, Mark," she shrugged. "It's just that I'm so confused. If I do what I think I should, it will be wonderful and good things will happen, but it may also be unpleasant, at first, and some people might not understand, or…or be – upset, as well."

His expression changed. The anger faded, and was replaced by puzzlement – and then, dawning certainty. He pressed her hands warmly between his. "I think I know what you're trying to tell me, Mima," he said intently. "And I think you should do what you think is right, no matter what. And you don't need to be scared, not of anything. Not while I'm around."

He pulled her hands toward him. "Can't you tell me what you're afraid of, Mima? What – what decision you have to make?"

Jemima shook her head unhappily. "I-I can't, Mark. I'm sorry, not yet. But it's preying on my mind so. I don't like what I'll have to do."

His eyes were full of compassion. "Of course not. But you shouldn't let that keep you from doing what you think is best."

Jemima looked up into his eyes. "Oh, Mark, it's such a comfort to talk to you," she cried. "I haven't been able to talk to anyone about this – it's been all bottled up inside me, until I think I'm going to–"

But it was as far as she got.

Mark simply pulled her hands behind him, and then put his own around her, and before she knew what was happening, he was kissing her.

His lips were warm, and tender, almost reverent, but she shook her head and pulled away. She looked up at him almost in despair, and opened her mouth, as if to say something, but then shook her head.

"Just kiss me, Mark," she told him. "Kiss me hard!"

CHAPTER NINE

Jemima kept to herself, and said little to anyone, for days after the bake sale. She was usually very quiet and peaceful, never one to nurse anger or to act out like her sister. But to Jemima's dismay, all that had unexpectedly changed – because now she was angry and upset.

She was trying to stay away from other people because she was horrified by the idea that she might bark at someone, like her sister Deborah. She was angry with the Englischer, she was angry with herself, she was angry with Mark and Samuel and Joseph, and she was even angry at her parents – with her father, for grabbing every decision out of her hands, and even with her poor mother, for wearing herself out in a useless gesture that would help no one.

Because in spite of her confusion, one thing at least was depressingly clear: despite of all their neighbors' hard work, the total proceeds that the Yoders would receive from the bake sale had only been 351 dollars and 43 cents. About what it would cost for Adam Yoder's parents to take him to a doctor...once.

The Yoders were like every other Amish family – they didn't participate in traditional health insurance. And if their Amish neighbors couldn't help them, they had no way to pay their medical bills. Who had that kind of money?

Except...her?

It was on her now. She was the only one who could help the Yoders, and therefore she had a moral obligation to do it. The preacher had been right; it was sinful for her to have the means to help her neighbors and to do nothing, just because she dreaded the process of selling that letter, or the people she'd have to deal with.

But why did it have to be her? Why did she have to find that cursed letter? Why couldn't it have gone to someone else – anyone else?

She had no head for business, and no interest in business. She had no desire to go among the Englisch or to be rich. She was horrified by that crazy Englischer, and appearing in a newspaper – on purpose – well, it was the opposite of what a good Amish person should do.

Jemima mulled these things over uneasily as she sat, well hidden, in the loft of her father's barn. It was where she always ran to hide when she'd been small, and it was still a good place for that. Because since she'd grown up, and grown pretty, no one ever suspected that she'd ever return to such a dusty corner.

But it was perfect for thinking. It was quiet and cool and sweetly fragrant of hay. She closed her eyes and rested her head against a big bale.

She'd hoped that Mark would help her find a way out when they had talked at the bake sale, but she'd been disappointed. Or maybe she had just been naïve. It wasn't Mark's fault that he wasn't a mind reader – it was hers, for expecting him to be one.

She had sought advice from him because he was a childhood friend – as if she could hide from her problems by going back to the past. But Mark was no longer a child, and neither was she.

And because they were courting, he'd naturally assumed that she'd been talking about her choice of a mate, and had been anxious to show his sympathy. He'd tried to make love to her because they were alone, and because his way of expressing affection was almost purely physical.

She sighed, and was momentarily distracted by an old

grievance.

If only Mark would tell her that he loved her – just once! – instead of expecting physical closeness to say it all!

Because what did a kiss mean, anyway? It could mean anything, unless the person doing the kissing bothered to explain what it meant.

But that was another worry, a distraction that she didn't have the luxury to dwell on.

Her problem now, was the letter.

There was no getting around her duty. She had to call the Englischer, accept his help and sell the letter. It was a fate she dreaded, but there was one thing that was even worse – the thought of little Adam Yoder, and others like him, suffering for lack of the medical care that she could easily provide.

If she could only work up the nerve to do what she must.

Jemima looked out through a chink in the barn wall, out toward the garden. It was drowsing peacefully under a quiet summer sun.

She hated the thought of her home being invaded by strangers, of being stalked by some crazy, greedy newspaper reporter that she didn't know and didn't want to know.

It was true that he was very handsome, with that big bush of sandy brown hair. It was streaked with all different colors of brown and blond, like the sun had bleached it out, but not all the same.

And his eyes were bright and blue, and his eyebrows were bushy and wild and moved as if they were alive.

And he did have a strong chin, nice white teeth, and a strong…mouth.

A slow wave of heat crawled from her feet to the top of her head. She couldn't help it, the memory came surging back, of his mouth clamped down over hers, and how that had felt.

An electric thrill flashed up her spine and branched out into little tingling, sparkling threads along every nerve in her body. She shuddered, and shook her head and frowned. She had been kissed many times before, and by many boys. But she had never, never been kissed by a madman.

It terrified her.

It was true that he had apologized, looked sorry, and even called her *the most beautiful girl he'd ever met.*

Jemima put her chin on her knees and hugged them.

Then she frowned. But her mother was right, a man's actions were what counted, and the Englischer was a madman, and a wicked one, to treat her so disrespectfully.

She opened her eyes, and the look in them was troubled. But if so – then she must also be mad, and wicked. Because when the Englischer had taken her in his arms and kissed her, she had been – electrified.

She frowned again, and her mouth moved in silent prayer. But when she opened her eyes, she had no sense of the presence of God, and was downcast about it.

Maybe her heart wasn't right any more.

That made it all the more awkward and terrifying to call that madman, and to talk to him again. Because, with her own feelings so jumbled up, surely she should stay as far away from him as she could get?

She chewed her thumbnail. Maybe she should just tell her father everything, and let him deal with the Englischer. That would be safest, and perhaps best.

But even though she knew it was right, somehow – she couldn't bring herself to do it.

Her father would take the letter and the decision out of her hands, just as he always did. And that would be the end. But for once in her life, Jemima thought, she wanted to be the one to decide. Even if that meant that she had to take a risk and do something that other people might not understand.

Something that she, even, might not fully understand.

She bit her lip, looking out through the little chink in the wall, out to the garden. But the idea of seeing the reporter again made her very uneasy. There was no knowing what he'd do. That mad Englischer always surprised her.

Always.

He frightened her, he shocked her, he made her angry, and he amazed her.

And what was even more unsettling – maybe she liked that, just a little bit.

Jemima's beautiful eyes widened in fear. She frowned, pulled her knees to her chest and prayed even more earnestly.

CHAPTER TEN

Jemima craned her neck to peer out of the little window in the phone shack, but her father was nowhere in sight. She closed her eyes and drummed one foot nervously against the wall.

The phone rang and rang. Six times, seven times, eight. No one was answering.

The sudden click of the receiver made Jemima's heart jump up into her throat, and she almost dropped the phone when a voice on the other end said, cheerfully:

"It's a beautiful morning at Uncle Bob's Amish Motel. My name is Stessily. How can I help you today?"

Jemima swallowed hard, and forced herself to answer:

"Good – good morning, Stessily. I – I'm calling for a Mr. – a Mr. Brad Williams. Is he in?"

"Hmm, let me see." There was a tapping sound on the other end. "Brad Williams. Oh – oh, I'm sorry, miss. It looks like he just checked out this morning. But it was only a few minutes ago – if you can wait, I'll see if he's still here."

"Thank you," Jemima replied faintly. She hardly knew what to hope for – that she would catch the crazy Englischer, or that he'd be gone forever.

She had fought herself for days, had prayed earnestly, and had tried to look at the thing from every angle. And in the end she had just decided to call the Englischer, and pray that somehow, everything worked out in the end.

Not that it was likely to work out.

She could hear the girl's voice faintly in the background, calling. "Mr. Williams – Mr. Williams!" There was unintelligible discussion, and within seconds, loud fumbling on the other end. Then, suddenly, the voice she had learned to dread:

"Miss King?"

Jemima bit her lip in irritation. She'd caught the Englischer. Just her luck!

"Yes."

There was a small pause. "Thank you for calling back," he

said quietly. To her intense relief, and for once, he sounded almost…sane.

"I know that couldn't have been easy for you. And I promise, nothing – unprofessional – will ever happen again." There was a sound like a deep breath on the other end of the line.

"Now. How can I help you?"

Jemima's heart was pounding, and the little shack felt hot – like it was closing in on her.

"You-you said that I needed to sign some papers," she said evenly.

"Yes, you must give the auction house written permission to sell the letter."

"Will you send them to me in the mail?"

"I can, if you like."

Jemima nodded. "Yes."

There was more fumbling. "If you'll give me your address…"

Jemima recited the information with her eyes squeezed shut. In spite of little Adam Yoder, and the preacher's message, she had the awful feeling that she was doing something wrong somehow, and that it was going to blow up on her.

That feeling intensified when the reporter added: "And once Brinkley's has the signed papers, they can prepare for the auction. An auction is always very exciting, and this one – well, it'll be historic. One in a million."

There was another pause, and he added: "It'd be a shame to miss it."

Jemima shook her head, and said, in a strangled voice: "I will only sign the papers. I can't go to any auction!"

The tone of the reporter's voice was suggestive of a shrug. "Why not?"

Jemima pulled the receiver away from her ear and stared at it. She sputtered: "You-you don't know anything about Amish people, about what we believe!" she cried, and slammed the phone down on the hook. Then she gathered her skirts and ran back up the hill, but not to hide inside the house.

To run into the barn, climb up into the loft, and curl up in the shadows, and be upset and confused – again.

Brad Williams heard the click on the other end of the line, and handed the receiver back to the grinning receptionist.

He grinned back, crookedly, gathered the shreds of his dignity about him, and limped back out to the truck.

But when he closed the door behind him, he just leaned his head against the rim of the wheel. There was only one thought pounding in his brain: She called back. She called back. She called back.

He just sat there, basking in his absurd joy. Because he was no longer ruined. He was no longer even on probation. He had his job and future back, and he still had a toehold on the story of the year.

The Duchess had called him back.

He flipped the knob on the radio and turned the volume up to blasting, beat his palms on the wheel, and sang at the top of his lungs like a lunatic all the way back to his apartment.

Once he was there, he flopped down on his couch with a bottle of soda in one hand and the phone in the other. Since the Ledger was springing for the sale fees, and had a hand in the negotiations, he was going to have to light a fire under Dapper Dwayne and get all this stuff fast tracked: the contract, the insurance forms, the commission agreements for the auction house, all the fine print.

He punched the necessary numbers on his phone, but to Brad's annoyance, the lawyer was out; he could only get his voicemail. But he was determined to get the show on the road as fast as humanly possible. It could take Brinkley's months to get such a huge auction advertised and scheduled.

And in the meantime, he had to be busy as well, keeping

the lines of communication open between him and Jemima, so that when the time came, she'd maybe agree to attend the auction.

He already knew how he was going to do it. He wouldn't send her everything at once. He'd take her one form at a time, and deliver them himself. He was sure he could come up with some excuse that was at least plausible.

That would give him time to establish rapport, and hopefully, trust. Once that groundwork was laid, then he could bring up the subject of the article – and the photo.

What had she said – something like: "You don't understand what the Amish believe"?

He sipped his drink. It was a fair enough criticism – it was true. Maybe if he learned a little more, he could couch his requests in a way that would make the Duchess more likely to say yes.

Maybe even to requests that had nothing to do with letters or a million dollars or auctions.

He punched a few buttons on his phone and said: "Amish religion."

The little screen winked to life and pulled up a long list of links. Brad punched another button, took a long draught of his soda, and began to read.

CHAPTER ELEVEN

Brad spent the rest of that day, and a good part of that night, absorbing the long – and to him – depressing history of the Amish. They had been a minority religious sect in Europe, and had been tortured and murdered because of it. They came to the New World looking to escape religious persecution.

Brad pushed a pile of crumpled clothes off his bed. Then he stretched out on it in the dark and learned about the Amish by the blue light of his smart phone.

It was not the usual immigrant story.

The Amish settled mainly in the northeastern states, where they withdrew from the larger world because of their belief that it was "wicked" and that they were called by God to be "separate."

Brad pulled a hand over his jaw ruefully. *Great.* He was a part of the world. So, to Jemima, he was starting out wicked. He was wicked by definition.

But, on the other hand, that could work to his advantage. Some girls had a thing for bad boys.

In fact, maybe he should encourage that perception. He took a pull at the bottle and read on:

Farming and close-knit communities were integral to the Amish faith and way of life, and as 19th-century society embraced technological changes, the Amish began to reject certain advances as disruptive to the way of life that they had chosen.

Essentially, if a new gadget or technology tended to pull people, and especially families, away from one another, it was rejected.

If an advance put their community in direct contact with the wicked outside world – it, too, was rejected.

They largely rejected telephones until the 20th century and in many communities, still only allow them in "phone shacks" out at the end of the road, rather than inside the house, because phones are considered disruptive to family life, and are a line to the outside world. Television is still verboten for the same reasons. Cars are disallowed, because they give *families the mobility to travel great distances and present them with the temptation to abandon their extended families and neighborhoods.*

Brad and shook his head.

But even in these circumstances, many Amish communities make concessions: owning a car is forbidden, but riding in one is not, if it belongs to someone else. Electric power is forbidden, because electric lines are a direct link to the outside world; but solar power is not, because solar panels are self-contained.

Change in Amish communities happens slowly, if at all. Amish families are strictly traditional, with the man the undisputed head of the household, and a high value placed on the qualities of submission and modesty, not just for the women and girls, but generally. Divorce is discouraged and rare.

Brad's eye jumped to the section marked courtship. He raised his brows.

Teenagers of 16 and older enter a period called rumspringa, in which they are allowed to go out and experience the wider world before joining the church. Rumspringa is often a time of courtship. But this time of latitude is mainly offered as a way of giving the young a chance to make an informed choice about joining the church. Because, once a new member joins the Amish church, and takes their vows to God, serious and repeated infractions could result in shunning, and/or excommunication.

Brad ran a hand through his hair. So, if that was right, Jemima was, technically, on her rumspringa and eligible to be courted. From what he'd seen, that was already well under way. He'd seen her with one guy already, and a girl as beautiful as the Duchess was sure to have others.

But if what he'd seen was representative, she probably wasn't committed to any of them. They were probably good little Mamma's boys, and chicks never went for that.

He looked down at the article. According to its author, Jemima was also eligible to go out into the world and walk on the wild side. So to speak.

Brad grinned in the dark, thinking *I can arrange that.*

He might even be able to use it as leverage when it came time to really pitch for the photo. After all, he could say, you're on your rumspringa. It's now or never!

The now or never tactic got good results generally with girls. He'd have to remember this useful variant, for later.

He went back to the article.

The Amish believe the major tenets of traditional Christianity, but with emphasis on showing, rather than telling. They do not proselytize, at least not heavily, and place great emphasis on meekness, non-violence, submission to

God, prayer, and hard work.

Brad flicked the phone off and tossed it onto his bedside table. He didn't really need to hear all that religious stuff. He thought he had a pretty good picture now. Good enough for what he wanted, anyway.

He put his arms behind his head and stared up at his bedroom ceiling. In a way, he was going to have a hard time getting his head around this Amish thing. It was as far removed from his own life as one pole was from another.

He tried to imagine what it would be like to live that life: to get up and dress in pilgrim clothes, and work in the fields like 100 years ago, and not even to have electricity. Poor Jemima! He felt sorry for her. No normal life. No pretty clothes, like a beautiful girl should have, no schooling past the eighth grade. No future, except the drab existence of a farm wife, condemned to wash clothes by hand and have a baby every year.

Thank heaven, maybe the letter would change that for her. At least, he hoped so. Maybe when Jemima understood that she had choices now, she'd choose to move away and live like a normal human being.

Still, he had to admit that there were some parts of her life that were pretty. Or at least, seemed pretty: the beautiful countryside where they all lived, with those endless, rolling green fields full of corn, and the antique farmhouses, and the buggies.

Even the way her old man stood guard over her, like a giant Rottweiler.

He sputtered and reached for a cigarette. That part must be nice. He wouldn't know, because his own old man had left when he was five, and his mother had drugged herself into a coma – and him into foster care – by the time he was nine.

He pulled his lips down. She was dead now, and he didn't know if his old man was still alive or not. Not that he cared.

He allowed himself to wonder what it would be like having parents that actually did the fifties sitcom trip.

He laughed to himself and amended: No, the pioneer trip.

That part, he imagined, would be very nice. It would feel comforting and safe. And in the 21st century, that was a real luxury. Maybe it helped make up for the other things they were missing.

The religious part was a big minus, though – all that praying. They sang hymns that were hundreds of years old for hours. It was as if they were always repenting for something.

It made him angry, suddenly. A sweet, sheltered girl like Jemima – what did she have to repent for? But then, religion was only good for putting guilt trips on people who didn't deserve them. The world would be a better place if everyone forgot all that stuff and became agnostic, like he was.

It'd be a happier place, anyway.

Brad finished the cigarette, crushed it out on the table, and yanked off his shirt. He turned over and flicked a few buttons on the phone, and music blared from the speaker until he drifted off to sleep.

But his thoughts continued into his dreams that night. He saw himself running through an Amish cornfield, chasing a beautiful redheaded girl whose tempting smile was always half-hidden, and just out of reach.

CHAPTER TWELVE

A week later, Brad began the first of a series of carefully-planned visits to Jemima's house. They were intended to help him build up friendship, trust, and eventually, an interview.

His first visit was a Hail Mary, and could have ended disastrously, but luck was with him. He arrived in the middle of the day, when the Duchess' old man was out somewhere, and she was working outside again.

It had been hard to get out to her place without attracting attention, but lucky for him, the place adjoined a piece of public land, an overgrown forest tract owned by the county. He had simply parked on the other side of that property, and hiked over.

By the time he had slogged to the edge of her family's farm, his slacks were torn by briars and he was covered in cockleburs.

He took a minute to pick the little prickly pods off of his clothing, before climbing over the fence.

He kept to the edge of the tree line, being careful not to walk out over the lawn. He had learned that the old man was a blacksmith and that if he was home, you could hear him from a distance away, but the house was quiet.

The red giant was gone.

Brad kept behind the bushes, working his way back to the spot where he had met Jemima before. It was an ideal hiding spot; he could see the whole house and garden without being seen himself. He returned to it, and sure enough, there was the Duchess, sitting in a little folding chair on one side of the garden. There was another, empty chair facing her.

He shot a glance at the house. The best he could tell, a big line of flowering bushes screened Jemima from the house, so if he stepped out from his hiding place, he should be safe, unless–

He ducked down. Unless, she had a visitor.

He crouched low, cursing softly under his breath. Some pretty farm boy had come out to see her. He sat down in the empty chair facing Jemima.

Brad grimaced. The guy was actually wearing a straw hat.

He was close enough to hear what they were saying, though he devoutly wished he wasn't because, of course, the guy was trying to romance the Duchess, and it was painful to watch.

The hat guy gave her a piece of paper. Brad craned his neck, wondering what it was.

Jemima looked up at him and smiled. "Oh, Joseph, another poem! This is so sweet," she murmured.

Brad shook his head. You're dying, buddy, he told the stranger. Sweet is for babies and lapdogs.

The guy looked down at his hands, as though he couldn't bring himself to lift his eyes to her face. "Read it, Jemima," he pleaded.

She looked startled, and Brad shook his head. Poor girl!

She cleared her throat, and coughed. "You are like a…strong mare, with a shiny red coat."

She looked up at him doubtfully, but he nodded encouragement, and she continued: "You are a hard worker, and work well with others. Yoke and…harness will be no hardship for you, because you are mild and gentle."

Brad laughed out loud, and Jemima's head jerked up suddenly. "What was that? Did you hear something, Joseph?"

Joseph shook his head, and his eyes returned to the paper.

She scanned the bushes again, and continued, less placidly: "Your road will be smooth and happy, and you will never run it alone."

Jemima finished, and looked up at the young man. "That's a – that's a lovely poem, Joseph."

Brad made a decision, and stood up suddenly. He stepped boldly onto the lawn, waved the forms over his head, and pointed to them.

Jemima's eyes met his over her visitor's shoulder. She shrieked and dropped the paper, and Brad ducked back into the bushes.

Joseph looked almost as alarmed as Jemima. He jumped up, and then sat down again, abruptly.

"What's wrong, Mima?" he asked earnestly.

Jemima's eyes scanned the bushes crazily. "I-I thought I saw something!" she stammered.

The young man turned and looked in the direction of her gaze. "I don't see anything, Mima," he said, in a puzzled tone. He turned back to her. "Maybe – you're a little nervous." The thought seemed to please him; he smiled a bit.

"Was I too – too ardent?"

Jemima uttered a choking sound that she abruptly

swallowed, and then pressed a hand to her head. "No, no, Joseph! It's just that – well, maybe you're right, I am a bit nervous today. I'm sorry."

Her visitor smiled serenely. He dared to pat her hand. "That's all right," he told her. "I won't press you, Jemima."

Jemima raised her head and cast a fiery look at the bushes. "I wish everyone had your courtesy, Joseph!" she cried.

He stood up, hat in hand. "May I call on you again – Mima?"

She was still looking out into the trees. "Yes, yes. Anytime you like! I mean – well, you'll have to ask my Daed." She raised her voice. "He'll be back any minute!"

Joseph nodded. "There's no hurry, Mima. I'll see you at worship Sunday." He leaned forward, and paused.

Jemima looked up at him, bit her lip, and allowed him to kiss her cheek.

After her visitor had disappeared around the side of the house, climbed into his buggy, and driven off down the road, she turned to the bushes, hands on hips.

Brad stepped out of them, laughing crazily.

"How dare you come out here when I told you not to!" Jemima cried, eyes blazing. "And you spied on me! How can you stand there laughing! You should be ashamed of yourself!"

Brad wiped his eyes and shook his head. "I'm sorry, Jemima," he sputtered. "I wasn't trying to spy, and I didn't mean to listen. I just didn't want to interrupt. I came out to bring you the auction contract. I figured it would be faster and safer than mailing it."

"Leave this minute!" she told him, pointing back to the bushes. "I specifically told you not to come. Don't you pay attention to anything that other people say?"

Brad raised his hands in the air. "Okay, okay," he shrugged. "Though it isn't very polite to insult me, after I took the trouble to make a special trip all the way out here."

That line of reasoning seemed to give her pause. Some of the fire died out of her eyes. She sputtered, "Just, just go now, before my father comes home. Because this time, I won't protect you!"

Brad looked up at her sharply, and grinned. She gasped, went beet red, stamped her foot, turned, and ran.

Brad set the contract down on the neatly-mown lawn, turned, and beat a strategic retreat. Because if there was any chance that she was right, he had better demonstrate the better part of valor.

Before he experienced the better part of a thrashing.

CHAPTER THIRTEEN

Jemima sat out on the front porch steps, looking up at the stars.

It was two o'clock in the morning, and she'd have to be up again at five, but she had long since given up any hope of getting any sleep.

That Williams fellow had popped up again in the bushes, for the third straight time in the last month. The first time, it had caused her to scream out, because Joseph was there, and she'd been terrified that Joseph would see the fellow standing there. The second time, he appeared early one morning, and

Deborah had almost caught them talking, and that would've been a disaster, because Deborah would gleefully have blabbed all she knew. But he was quick – she had to give him that. He had dived into the bushes like an expert.

It made her wonder if he had a lot of experience hiding in bushes outside girl's houses.

This last time had been at dusk, just before it was time to go inside. He had been bold enough to come out onto the lawn this time, and he had come quite close in the near-darkness. Uncomfortably close, really. She put a hand to her brow, and smoothed back a little wisp of hair. He had stood so close that she could feel his breath, and catch the scent of his clothes; they had been faintly fragrant of pipe tobacco, and that man scent. She couldn't quite describe it – it was a clean scent, equal parts salt, and soap, and skin.

She sighed and rubbed her arms against the evening chill.

He had wanted her to sign a paper. Every time he'd come out to the house, it was the same thing: sign this paper.

She bit her lip and looked up at the sky unhappily. It was odd that he didn't bring all the papers at the same time and have done with it. And she really should have told him to go away and never come back. He didn't listen, he was stubborn beyond all reason, and she was terrified that someone would see him, and ask her why he was there.

She couldn't figure that out, herself.

Unless, he wanted to be near her, like he'd said once.

She twisted the end of her long braid. She didn't like the way things were going. There was going to be trouble if things went on the way they were going.

She was beginning to understand that she'd been naïve to think she'd be able to keep the sale of the letter a secret. Once the reporter knew about it, well, she was pretty much ruined, and she had been silly not to admit that before now.

He had already gotten the story out of her – how she'd found the letter, what it had said, and even how she felt about what it had said.

She blushed, and looked down at her hands. How had he done that? She hadn't intended to tell anyone how beautiful she thought it was.

Maybe it was the way he had sat down beside her, and settled down and listened. The reporter boy listened better than anyone she had ever met.

Well, to her story at least. He didn't listen at all in the general way, when it came to things like keeping his distance and behaving like a gentleman. He had kept his promise, technically – the promise he had made to her in the store. He hadn't grabbed her up or tried to kiss her, or laid a finger on her, not even to shake her hand. He had been polite, and had stuck mostly to talking just about the letter, and the auction.

But he showed up at the house whether she liked it or not, he laughed at inappropriate things, and he was always nagging her to let him take a picture. He had said that the world would want to see the girl who found the million-dollar letter.

And, that he wouldn't mind having a picture of her, himself. Then he had smiled again, and winked.

She would have dismissed that as nonsense, except she'd caught him staring at her, and not just at her face, especially when he'd thought she was looking somewhere else. Jemima tossed her head and looked out over the slumbering fields.

He was a typical barbarian Englischer and had no manners whatsoever.

But, she had to admit, there was another side, too. Because when it had come time to tell her story, then he had gotten very quiet, and settled down and listened very hard. He listened with his mind, which was the best way she could put it. Not just with his ears.

He had smiled when she told him that she'd been glad the letter was real, because it was a beautiful letter – very sweet and romantic. He had a wonderful smile, it was very warm, and it lit up his face.

Like he really…understood.

She had actually dreamed about him. And that horrified her, but she supposed she didn't have any say over that – or responsibility. She wasn't in control of her dreams, after all.

She had dreamed that the Williams fellow had climbed in through her bedroom window and chased her all through the house, with her wearing nothing but a cotton shift and her hair going all down her back.

And then, then she dreamed that he caught her and kissed her again, hard, just like he had in the store that day. And she screamed, and he jumped out through a window again, and broke all the glass out of it, like a wild animal.

And then she dreamed that Mark and Samuel and Joseph came running into the room and gave her flowers, and since she couldn't decide between them, she married them all, right there in the living room, in her cotton gown.

But when she turned to leave with them, she looked back over her shoulder, and the Englischer's crazy blue eyes were watching her from the broken window.

She woke up with her heart pounding, and she must have cried out, because Deborah had called out from across the hall for her to shut up, and go back to sleep.

But she hadn't slept. She hadn't slept for hours.

She chewed her nail.

This last time when he'd shown up, the Williams fellow had come as close as she'd let him, and looked into her face with those bright eyes. He had said:

"Tomorrow is the auction, Jemima. I know you're reluctant to go, but please, give it serious thought. This is something that only happens once in a lifetime. You will never get a chance to see something this important again. It's – well, it's history – and it will change your life."

She had set her mouth, given him a direct look, and was on the point of telling him that it would not change her, but he had smiled, and nodded, as if to say "Yes, it will." He put out his hand, as if he would have taken her cheek in it, and then dropped it to his side.

He smiled, and added softly: "And Jemima, you shouldn't be afraid of that. It'll be a good thing."

Then he had added: "It's now – or never."

His voice had been as low and tender as if he had been talking to a baby. The memory of it made a ghostly tingle dance up her spine.

He wanted her to meet him in town tomorrow, and get into a car with him alone, and let him drive her to another city. It was unheard of – it was definitely not allowed – and if anyone ever found out that she did it, well, she couldn't imagine.

Only one thing was certain – it would be a scandal, and she would be in disgrace and very likely in trouble as well.

She bit her lip again and shook her head. There was definitely going to be trouble. Because she had already decided that she was going with him.

She believed that the end result was the will of God, and justified it to herself that way. But if she was really honest, she had to admit that she probably would have found a reason to do it anyway.

Because it was wicked and rebellious, but she wanted to see him again. She wanted to get to know him better.

Because only then could she get the answer to the question that had haunted her for months.

Why didn't you take that letter when I gave you the chance?

CHAPTER FOURTEEN

Just after four o' clock, Jemima freshened up and dressed. She could hear her parents stirring down the hall; they were always the first to rise.

She felt guilty already, because she was going to have to tell a story to explain why she was going to be gone all day. The best thing she could think of was to volunteer to deliver some preserves that her mother wanted taken to her sister, a few miles away. It was a long walk, and her parents would expect her to stay for some time, visiting her aunt, and then it would be a long walk back.

It was at least a plausible story, though she'd also have to make up a story about why she hadn't shown up at her aunt's house, as planned.

Jemima bit her thumbnail nervously, but to her dismay, there was nothing left – she had chewed it down to the quick. She knew that lying was wrong, but how could she possibly slip away for a whole day without giving her family some reason for going?

When she went down to the kitchen, her mother was already pouring out coffee, and her father was nursing a cup between his big hands.

Jacob looked up, and his expression softened. He grinned at his eldest daughter, but Jemima was stabbed by guilt, and could only muster a small, sickly smile in return. To her relief, he didn't seem to notice, and her mother pulled her aside.

"Jemima, start some bacon, please."

Jemima did as she was told, but shot her mother a surreptitious look as she carefully placed bacon strips into a fry pan. "Mamm – do you still want to send that basket of preserves to Aunt Priscilla? I could take them today, if-if you like."

Her mother looked at her. "Well – yes, I still do. I'd appreciate that, Jemima, if you're willing. But you'll have to walk. Your father is taking the buggy into town today."

"Oh, that's all right," Jemima answered quickly, and directed her attention to the stove. But when she raised her eyes again, she noticed that her sister, who had just arrived, was staring at her through narrowed eyes.

"Can I come with you?" Deborah asked suddenly.

Jemima's mouth dropped open slightly. Deborah never asked to come with her – anywhere.

Her mother smiled and nodded. "That's a wonderful idea, Deborah! Aunt Priscilla will be glad to see you."

Jemima bit her lip, and added slowly: "Yes! The last time I saw her, she told me that she wanted to teach you how to make her sauerkraut. Now you can learn!"

She didn't raise her eyes. That was another lie; she was getting in deeper and deeper.

But as she'd hoped, Deborah made a face and shrugged. "In that case, I'd rather stay here. I hate her sauerkraut!"

"Deborah!" cried both of her parents, at once.

Jemima finished the bacon, and helped her mother prepare the rest of breakfast. When everything was ready, she sat down meekly at the table, ate in silence, and kept her eyes mostly on her plate. She noticed, uneasily, that Deborah was watching her, and wondered if there was some look on her face that gave her away. Or – her blood ran cold at the thought – that she'd said something in her sleep that gave her away.

When breakfast was over at last – because to Jemima, it seemed to last forever – she lingered behind to receive the jars that she was supposed to be carrying to her aunt. Her mother looked at her in surprise.

"Why Jemima, do you mean to go now?" she asked.

Jemima looked up at her. "Yes. It'll take a while to get there. I'd like to get there before the sun gets too hot."

Her mother nodded. "That's sensible. Here, I'll get them for you."

Jemima was alarmed to see that Deborah stayed behind at the table as well. Her suspicious blue eyes were still watching. Jemima finally bit her lip, and met them. She gave her sister a direct look.

"Is there something you wanted to ask me, Deborah?" she said, trying to keep her tone neutral.

Deborah narrowed her eyes again, but shook her head. To Jemima's intense relief, she pushed off from the table and went back upstairs.

Her mother returned with a half-dozen jelly jars, a loaf of bread, and half a ripe cheese in a basket. "Here, take these to your aunt," she instructed, "and give her a kiss for me! Be sure to tell her that I'm going to return her book, as soon as I've finished reading it."

Jemima nodded submissively, and felt more wretched than

she could ever remember feeling in her life. Maybe she should just forget all about this thing.

But her mother was standing in front of her, with her hands on her hips.

"Well, scoot, girl!" she told her.

Jemima stood up, heart pounding, and carried the basket out through the front door. A rosy predawn light was in the east, and already the countryside was clearly visible. The sounds of early morning came faintly from across the valley: the sound of a barn door closing, a man calling to someone, a rooster's call.

Jemima moved quickly around the side of the house, and walked out to the garden. The Williams fellow had said that he'd be waiting for her in his usual place, but she'd learned that he was a very late riser. She had never seen him before 6 a.m., at any rate. But maybe this morning, he'd make a special effort.

He had promised to take her to his truck, and to drive her to the auction house. He had told her that it was scheduled at 9 o'clock, but the city was a good distance.

She walked out to the very edge of the garden. Her heart was pounding.

This was craziness. She shouldn't be travelling with a man she didn't know, not to the grocery store, much less to a city hours away. He was a crazy man, he'd proved it. What if he just drove away with her?

What if–

A soft hiss from the bushes brought her focus sharply back to earth. The branches trembled. Sure enough – there he was, just visible from her vantage point. She hesitated for a split-second, then walked quickly toward him, and followed into the underbrush.

But as she looked back over her shoulder, she was shocked to see that Deborah was standing on the front porch of the house, watching her as she went.

The Williams fellow took her hand and pulled her through the bushes until they reached the fence that separated the King farm from county land.

Then he turned to smile at her. He was beaming, and looked happier than she'd ever seen him.

"I knew you had it in you, Duchess!" he grinned.

Jemima frowned. "What did you call me?" she demanded.

"Duchess," he grinned, unrepentant. "You look like one. Now, we have to go over this field to get to my truck. I'll help you over the fence."

Jemima slapped his hand away. "I can climb over a fence by myself," she told him.

He grinned at her again, and waved toward it invitingly. Jemima set the heavy basket down in the weeds, hiked her skirt up, and climbed over. It was very awkward, and embarrassing, but she wanted to show this Brad Williams fellow that she was her own person, and not a helpless child.

Once she was over, he hopped over it easily, and then led her through the scrubby, overgrown field to a line of trees at the edge of the road. Sure enough, there was a white truck. He walked to the passenger side and opened the door for her gallantly. She gave him a long look before climbing in – carefully, and with great trepidation.

He walked quickly to the driver's side and climbed in. As he turned the switch, and the engine growled to life, he turned to her and smiled – that nice, warm smile.

Only – excited, too. She could see it.

"Don't worry, Duchess," he told her. "This is going to be the best day of your life."

As the truck pulled off down the road, Jemima shrank down in the seat, turning her face away from the window and covering it with her apron, in case she caught sight of anyone on the road.

If she was spotted riding in a car alone with an Englisch reporter, it was most definitely not going to be the best day of her life.

CHAPTER FIFTEEN

It only took fifteen minutes for the truck to leave the green hill country behind, and soon they were zooming down the highway on the way to the city. Jemima watched the traffic with terrified eyes. She had only been in a car a few times before, and then only when she'd been sick. The trip had always been to the clinic in town, which was only a few miles away from her house.

But now the truck was hurtling down a highway as broad and wide as the road to destruction at lightning speed, barely avoiding other cars and larger trucks that suddenly appeared in front of them. Jemima clutched the armrest with white fingers, and finally had to close her eyes.

The Williams fellow had been quiet, but he started to hum to himself. Jemima frowned. She was trying to pray.

Then he started talking. "Now, when we get there, Duchess, I'll take you back to the waiting area. I've requested a room for us, so we can watch the auction privately. They've printed up a brochure for the buyers, all about the letter and its history. That might be fun to look at, while you're waiting. The guy from the appraiser's told me last week that he thinks the bidding is going to be fierce. You can't count on that, but the lady from Brinkley's – Miss Juniper, you'll meet her today – said that interest has been off the charts."

Jemima turned to look at him. "My name is Jemima. Not Duchess!"

He grinned at her, and she frowned again. "You don't care what I think, do you, Brad Williams?" she asked crossly. "You just want a story, to make yourself famous!"

He nodded placidly. "Of course I want a story. It's my job to want a story," he agreed. "Is that unfair?"

Jemima was nonplussed. She had never heard anyone admit a self-interested motive so readily. But then, he was an Englischer, and couldn't be expected to do anything else.

"Have you eaten breakfast?" he asked pleasantly.

She turned and looked at him. "Yes."

"Good. It'll take us an hour to get there, so you might be

hungry again. I've arranged for a light brunch before the auction, in case you are."

He was watching the road, and so she let her eyes linger on him. He had combed his hair back neatly, but it was still a big wavy bush, with twigs sticking out at odd angles against the stark light. His eyebrows were like...really, like the fuzzy blonde worms she had played with as a child, always moving, and curling up and down. He had a strong profile: a straight nose, a square jaw, and a stubborn chin.

"Why didn't you keep the letter?" she blurted.

The question seemed to take him by surprise. The fuzzy eyebrows shot up.

"Why? Well, I–" He was silent for a long minute, looked at her keenly, and then smiled and shrugged. "You know, I think you've got me there, Duchess. I don't really know why not. I have a few guesses. Most of them having to do with pride." He turned again and looked at her.

"And some of them, having to do with impressing a gorgeous redhead."

Jemima felt her mouth falling open, and shut it. She turned her eyes to the road ahead, and stared at it steadfastly.

But when she was sure he wasn't looking, she allowed herself the tiniest ghost of a smile.

An hour later, they crossed the perimeter of the city. Jemima gazed up at the skyline in wonder, and more than a little fear. The glittering buildings, towering up into the sky, seemed unlovely and ominous to her. They seemed the very personification of hochmut – of human pride and arrogance. They reminded her of the Tower of Babel – an attempt to climb to heaven without God.

Brad Williams noticed the direction of her gaze. He smiled. "Great, huh? Brinkley's is next to the convention center downtown. We should be there in twenty minutes, and with a little time to spare."

They exited the highway and turned onto broad, congested city streets that, to Jemima, seemed even worse than the ominous buildings. They were alive with people – all of them passing each other without so much as a glance or a nod, and most of them frowning or preoccupied with their gadgets. Lights flashed on and off garishly. There were no trees, only huge signs. And the noise – horns honking, the roar of busses and trucks, and exhaust smells that filtered in even through the car's ventilation system.

She cast a worried glance at her companion, but he seemed completely untroubled by the ugliness of their surroundings.

He glanced at her briefly. "Mind if I smoke?"

She shook her head, and he lit a cigarette, and blew a puff of smoke toward the ceiling. "Now, when we walk in, let me do the talking."

Jemima frowned at him again. "I'll do my own talking," she informed him, and he grinned at her, in that infuriating way.

"No need to get your hackles up. It's just that they know me. I've talked to them before. I can run interference for you, but if you'd like, I can leave it all to you."

He looked at her again out of the corner of his eye, raised his bushy brows, and stuck the cigarette up toward the ceiling.

Jemima bit her lip, and repressed the sudden urge to kick the underside of the dashboard.

Just as he had predicted, fifteen minutes later, the truck dived deep into the bowels of the Brinkley's building. Or at least, that was how it seemed to Jemima. They entered a huge, dark parking deck, as black as any cave, and to her at least, twice as frightening. It echoed with phantom noises and voices, ghostly puddles of light hid more than they revealed, and the low ceiling made her intensely conscious that there were tons of steel and stone overhead. It was all she could do to keep herself from reaching out for the Englischer's arm.

He pulled the truck into a tiny space, turned the engine off, and turned to her, his bright blue eyes glowing in the half-light.

"Show time," he smiled. "Ready to go?"

Jemima looked up into his face fearfully. He winked at her again, and grinned, and it made her feel a little bit better.

But only a little.

She stayed close to him as they walked through the echoing darkness to the elevator. Brad Williams pushed a button and whistled, seemingly unconcerned. When the doors opened he stepped right in; but Jemima hesitated at the entrance.

"Don't be shy, Duchess," he told her wryly. "The only other alternative is the stairs – six flights."

Jemima bit her lip, and stepped in reluctantly.

As soon as the doors closed, there was a huge hum and Jemima put one hand out to steady herself against the wall as the floor vibrated.

Within seconds, the doors opened again. Just beyond them was a glittering lobby with silver chandeliers, walls of glass, plush furniture and deep red carpet.

Jemima barely repressed a gasp. She had never seen anything like it before in all her life. It looked like – like Nebuchadnezzar's palace in Babylon.

She walked closely behind Brad Williams as he led her to another bank of elevators, but much fancier than the one they had just left. Jemima noticed, with a rush of self-consciousness, that some of the passersby were staring at her. She put a hand to her cap.

The elevator doors closed behind them, and a little light on a console showed the floors as they passed, but this time there was hardly any sense of motion. The doors opened again.

This time, the doors opened onto a large, plush lobby ringed by entrances to smaller auction rooms. Jemima's companion led her out toward a large desk set up in the center of the room. A solitary woman sat behind it. Jemima noticed that she was young, smartly dressed in a business suit, and that her dark hair was swept back in a very professional looking updo.

She rose as they approached and smiled.

"Hello again, Mr. Williams," she beamed, and turned her eyes on Jemima. "And this must be Miss King? I'm Margo Juniper."

Jemima felt herself going red, but shook the well-manicured hand that the woman held out.

"Welcome to Brinkley's! We're so glad you decided to attend the sale, Miss King," Margo Juniper continued. "The auction will commence in thirty minutes, and the conference room is already full to overflowing. There's been incredible interest – we haven't seen anything like this letter in years."

Brad Williams turned to smile at her, and Jemima knew

that he was saying "See? I told you so."

"If you'll follow me, I'll show you back to the private room. There's a television in it, so you can watch the bidding as it happens. I've set up the brunch you ordered, Mr. Williams, but if there's anything else you'd like, just let me know."

"Thank you."

Brad held out his hand in silent invitation, and Jemima followed the woman across the opulent lobby to a small door off to one side. When she opened it and stepped back, Jemima's eyes widened.

The little private room was the last word in Englisch excess. Three leather couches ringed an antique table covered in food. There was juice and tea in crystal glasses, coffee in china cups, plates of sliced ham and cheese, croissants, a jelly caddy, what looked like tiny cucumber sandwiches, steaming scrambled eggs, crisp bacon, toast, and pancakes with syrup.

She looked back at Brad William's face almost in consternation. But he just smiled.

"It's perfect, Miss Juniper!" he told her. "You've outdone yourself. Thanks for everything."

"You're welcome. If you need anything, you can just call me from the phone on the side table – extension 1."

"Will do."

She smiled again. "It was nice to meet you, Miss King," she said pleasantly. "Good luck with the auction, and thank you again for allowing us to help you with the sale of such an important document."

Then the door closed behind her.

CHAPTER SIXTEEN

As soon as she was gone, Brad Williams plopped down on one of the couches and poured coffee into a china cup. Not for her, Jemima noted, with a twinge of irritation – for himself.

"Sit down, Duchess," he told her easily. He reached for a small remote on the table and switched on the television. Instantly the conference room materialized, and it was evident that Miss Juniper had told the unvarnished truth: every last seat in the auction room was taken, and dozens of people were standing against the walls.

Jemima stared at the screen, round-eyed. She could see everything, just as it was happening, in the room next door!

Brad Williams glanced at her face between bites of toast and teased: "What's the matter, Duchess, haven't you ever seen a T.V. before?"

Jemima turned her eyes to his face, and was gratified to see him look temporarily chagrined. "Oh-oh, yeah. Sorry, I forgot. Well, at any rate, we'll be able to watch the bidding. It should be a real smackdown. They all seem to want that letter bad."

Jemima frowned and sank down onto the couch.

It was nothing but greed, all of it. It felt wrong, and dirty somehow, and she had to remind herself that she was – thought she was – obeying a direct command from God.

But obeying God had never been so confusing before.

Brad Williams collected some of the tidbits onto a plate and handed them to her. "Go ahead, eat. The auction may last for a while, and once we're out of here, the only other chance you'll get is the drive thru somewhere. As much as I'd like to spoil you, I can't promise you a spread like this on the Ledger's expense account."

Jemima took the plate from him, and nibbled morosely on a piece of cheese. She became aware that he was watching her, and she returned his gaze unhappily.

Brad Williams brushed the crumbs off his fingertips and leaned forward across the table. His bright eyes were intent. "Look, Jemima – I know what a big step this is for you. It can't have been easy to come all this way, and…with me." He looked down, and then up at her again. "It has to feel way strange, and maybe a little scary. But trust me – it's going to be fine. Really."

Jemima looked at him uncertainly. His eyes were full of that warm, sympathetic look again. Like he really did understand. Maybe, maybe God was using this young man to accomplish His will, even though he was an Englischer.

Brad smiled at her again. "Because, Jemima King, in another hour, you're going to be the richest Amish woman in history."

Then he cracked the devil's own grin.

Jemima put her plate down with a clatter, and reverted to chewing her nails.

After they had finished eating, Brad Williams had lit yet another cigarette, and she had decided – twice – to just get up and leave, and then didn't, the auction started. A man walked out onto a small stage and set the letter, now mounted in a clear plastic stand, up for all to see. The people in the crowd craned their necks.

After he had gone, the auctioneer walked briskly to the podium. He was tall, slim, youngish, and very smartly dressed.

He got right to the point. "We have here Item Number 10 in the catalog, a letter from George Washington to his wife Martha."

Brad Williams turned to look at her, smiling. Jemima returned a faint, tepid smile and raised her eyes to the television screen.

"I'm going to start the bidding out at $50,000. Fifty thousand dollars. Fifty thousand, do I have fifty-five. Sixty. Sixty-fi– Seventy, thank you sir. Can I have eighty thousand? Eighty, eighty-five, ninety."

Jemima watched in dumbstruck amazement. The auction had just begun, and already she had more money than she could imagine. Why did all those people want the letter so badly? It was sweet, it was even historically important, but it was just a letter, after all!

And if those rich people were that foolish with money – how had they gotten rich in the first place?

"One hundred thousand. Do I hear one hundred fifty, one sixty, one seventy." The auctioneer nodded toward a woman who seemed not to have made any motion at all. "One hundred eighty thousand. One hundred ninety, can I have two hundred? Two hundred, two hundred twenty-five. Yes, sir."

The auctioneer nodded toward a man talking on the phone. The man looked up at him and nodded. "Two hundred fifty thousand."

Jemima closed her eyes and leaned back into the luxurious leather cushions. This wasn't happening. She had never more than half believed those appraisers, and certainly had doubted Brad Williams when he told her that she was going to be filthy rich. She had thought she might get enough to help Adam Yoder with his bills, and maybe a few other people; and, if she was frugal, she might be able to sock a little away for her own family, just in case of an emergency. But this–

When she opened her eyes again, the auctioneer was no longer talking, but chanting in a fast, nasal sing-song: "Five-hundred fifty, five hundred seventy-five, can I see six hundred?"

There was a momentary pause, and Jemima held her breath. The auctioneer's eyes swept the room.

Then he nodded. "Six hundred. Can I hear six-fifty? Six fifty. Six fifty. In the back. Six seventy-five, seven hundred!"

Jemima rolled her eyes to Brad William's face. He was sitting on the couch opposite with his elbows on his knees, and his hands clasped. He was staring up at the T.V. screen with a look of such undisguised pain that Jemima felt suddenly guilty. Yes, of course he looked sick. How could he not?

All of this could have been his.

He hadn't noticed that she was looking at him. He was looking up at the screen with longing in his eyes, but to her surprise, Jemima saw no hint of regret. What was that he had said – something about pride – and wanting to impress a gorgeous redhead?

She felt so sorry for him suddenly that before she realized what she was doing, on impulse, she reached out and gave his hand a sympathetic squeeze.

He took her hand without missing a beat, as if it had been the most natural thing in the world for her to offer, and continued to look up at the screen. Jemima's eyes followed his. The auctioneer was now talking so fast that she could barely make out what he was saying: "Nine hundred thousand, nine-fifty. Nine fifty – thank you ma'am. One million dollars. One million. One – the gentleman in the front."

Jemima felt her heart throbbing in her chest, and closed her eyes again. She was never going to be able to hide this; she'd been lying to herself to imagine that she could. She was going to go home a millionaire, just as the appraisers had predicted, and she was going to have to explain everything.

But would her family understand?

And even more urgent – would Mark and Samuel and Joseph?

She shook her head, frowning. She would have to explain to her parents, and then most likely to the bishop. None of this was allowed, none of it had even happened to anyone else, and she was most likely going to have to repent.

She ticked off the list of infractions in her head. First and most glaringly, running off alone with an Englischer, meeting with him secretly beforehand, and not telling her parents about him at any point in that process. Then, not telling the bishop. Keeping the letter a secret, and not asking anyone else if she should sell the letter. Lying to her parents about going to her aunt's.

She opened her eyes. And watching a television.

She felt suddenly ill.

The auctioneer's voice rattled on: One million two hundred thousand. One million three. Thank you. One million four, one million five. One million six. One million six. Anyone?"

He looked around the room. "One million six. Last call. One million six." He brought a small gavel down with a bang,

Sold!" he announced, and the crowd broke out into applause.

Jemima stared at the screen in open-mouthed disbelief. One-million-six-hundred-thousand dollars.

She was dimly aware that Brad Williams was hugging her, and saying "Congratulations Duchess."

Then the door to the room suddenly burst open, and a camera flash went off.

CHAPTER SEVENTEEN

Brad Williams jumped up from the couch and thrust himself between Jemima and the intruder, but it was too late. His photographer had popped off five shots before he even had a chance to put up a hand.

He glanced quickly at Jemima, then scowled at the newcomer, and leaned in close to hiss: "Eddie, what're you doing? I told Delores I'd get the picture. She promised to do this my way!"

The young man smiled at Jemima, and then replied, through his teeth: "Delores says she gave you until the end of the auction. The auction is over. And so is this story, hot shot. Wrap things up, so we can run it!"

Brad's eyes widened. "Is Delores here?"

The photographer's lips pinched into a smug smile.

Brad ran a distracted hand through his hair. "Oh, no. Oh–" He grabbed the man's arm. "Is she outside now?"

"She called me from the parking deck. She's on her way up."

Brad frowned, looked down at the floor, and then hissed: "Go out and stall her for me!"

"Why?"

"Just do it. Or next week I'll write a series called '500 uses for pig dung' and send you out to Duluth for a 10-page spread!" He shoved the man's shoulder, and the photographer crashed against the door, shot him an evil look, and left.

Then he closed his eyes, took a deep breath, and turned back to Jemima.

Her green eyes were two big question marks. "Who was that? Why did he take my picture when I told you I–"

Brad ignored her. He sat down quickly on the couch and punched the button on the phone. Maybe he could get Jemima out of there before Delores arrived and picked her brain like a mad scientist.

"Hello, Margot? This is Brad Williams." He looked up at Jemima and tried to smile reassuringly. "Miss King has to go now, but she wanted to leave by a private exit.

"You understand – she doesn't want to be approached by the curious. Yes. Yes, I'll be happy to. No, we're in something of a hurry."

The secretary's voice buzzed faintly. "Really?" He looked at another door on the opposite end of the room. "Clever! And thanks, gorgeous. I owe you."

He put the phone down with a clatter and rose. "Well, that just about wraps it up, doesn't it, Duchess?" he said brightly, his eyes on the door. "There's a private exit, so you don't have to talk to anyone else."

Jemima frowned at him. "What's going on? You told me–"

Brad took her arm, pulled her smoothly to her feet, and propelled her across the room to the alternate doorway. He opened it and gave her just enough of a nudge to send her through.

The sound of the other door opening gave him just enough time to shut the door behind her, and lean against it, before the door to the outer hallway opened, and Delores Watkins walked in.

Brad crossed his arms. "Well, Delores – I didn't expect you here! How was the air traffic coming down Main Street?"

The older woman ignored him. She put her camera down on a small table and looked around. "Where's the girl?"

Brad shrugged. "You just missed her."

Delores' mouth thinned to an annoyed line. "Hmm... I wanted to get a juicy angle to pull in the millennials. Something about her love life. If she has one."

Brad raised his brows in mock regret. "Yeah, that's a shame. I just sent her back to 1845."

Delores gave him a narrow look. "On the Ledger expense account, I suppose."

Brad shrugged again, and smiled.

"Well, since she's gone, make yourself useful. What was the final sale price for the letter?"

Brad's smiled deepened. "One million six."

Delores nodded, and seemed mollified. "Good. Your story is ready to go, and now we have the photos. But I'd like to do a follow-up, if the story does well. And after what it's cost us – it had better do well."

Brad felt rotation in the small of his back. The doorknob behind him was turning. He leaned against it and laughed loudly.

"Trust me, Delores. Who loves you?"

Delores raised her heavily-lined brows and snorted. "The better question would be: who delivers? It had better be you, golden boy, if you want to grow up to be a real reporter."

"It can't miss, D. Fifty says a million hits before it's all over."

Delores shook her head and turned to the door. "You don't have fifty, Diamond Jim."

On this crushing parting shot, she departed.

He closed his eyes and slumped against the door, but the knob began digging into his lower back again. He turned and opened it.

Jemima stood in the opening, hands on hips. Her lovely eyes were bright with indignation.

"Why did you lie to that woman?" she demanded. "And why did you lie to me? You said you weren't going to take my picture!"

Brad stepped through the doorway, closed the door behind him, and ushered her down a narrow hall. "Trust me, if you knew Delores, you would understand instantly. And I didn't take your picture. That was my morally deficient colleague, without my knowledge or consent." He opened a door at the far end, which opened out to face a private elevator.

He pressed a button, and then turned to face her. "When I see him again, I'll object in the strongest possible terms."

The elevator doors opened, and he nudged her into the

elevator. "I just talked to Margot Juniper, and she says that Brinkley's will transfer the money to the bank account you gave them within 30 days. It will be one million six, less any applicable taxes, and of course, Brinkley's fees."

To his relief, this intelligence had the effect of silencing Jemima's objections. She frowned, looked worried, and began to chew a pink fingernail.

The elevator took them down to the garage level, and the door slid open soundlessly. They were in a glass-walled bay facing the parking deck.

He turned back to her. "Just stay here and I'll bring the truck around. That way, no one will see you walking out."

"Why are you scared that someone will see me?" Jemima objected. "I'm not hiding from anyone!"

"Of course not," he smiled, over his shoulder. "I'll be right back."

He walked quickly through the underground garage, weaving between cars and looking over his shoulder. The word was out now, and–

He slowed down, cursing under his breath. Sure enough, there was a gang of older reporters waiting for him around the white truck.

He looked down at the floor; but when he looked up again, he had firmly adjusted his game face and was smiling broadly. He sauntered out into the light, hands in pockets.

"Well, well! Am I throwing a party?"

Five hungry faces turned toward him. "There he is! Where's your little friend, junior? The Amish princess?"

"Oh, now, that's a sad story, friends. She left me for a guy with a beard." He fumbled in his pockets for the keys. "She said I wasn't hot enough."

"Come on, now, Brad. What happened to her? We'd like to get acquainted."

"She beat it back to the green hill country. Though I did my best to get her to run away with me."

They laughed. "Your sugar momma?"

"My insurance plan."

The reporters laughed again. "Too bad, Brad! Care to give the rest of us a shot?"

"You're on your own. I suggest you find some dungarees from the Civil War."

Another reporter leaned in and jabbed him in the chest. "You know where she lives. Come on now, tell us."

Brad smiled up into the other man's eyes. "I know where she used to live. With a million bucks in her bank account, I don't think she's going back to the farm. She did say something about going to a hotel, though."

"Which hotel?"

"Where? Here?"

Brad slid into the truck and closed the door behind him. He leaned out of the window. "I don't know. I'm off to indulge my grief. Anybody wanna loan me a twenty?"

They waved him away. "As if! Get out of here."

Brad cranked the truck and pulled away slowly. As soon as he had straightened the truck, rounded the corner, and the last reporter had faded from the rearview, he turned the truck sharply and made a beeline back to the private landing.

Jemima was still standing there patiently, and to his relief, she was alone. He leaned over and pushed the door open.

She hesitated again, bit her lip, and then slid in.

CHAPTER EIGHTEEN

He drove out of the parking deck as fast as he could, and did a few switchbacks on the city streets just in case some of those guys had spotted them. And was glad he did; while they were waiting at a light, he saw Channel 4's van go gliding down a side street like a shark patrolling the shallows. He nodded grimly. *Yes, their star reporter, Andrews: he was a smart one.* But, judging from the way Andrews was scanning the convention center, it looked like the little weasel had bought his story about the hotel.

And so he'd been thrown right off the scent by a college intern who wasn't even a real reporter yet. Brad exhaled with a sigh, and scanned the rearview. To his relief, he didn't see anyone else, but he didn't relax until he'd cleared downtown and was on the highway again.

Because he knew what would happen if one of his rivals got hold of Jemima. They'd dissect her like a lab specimen, and then spin every innocent thing she might say in the most sensational terms possible. God knew, he wasn't the most ethical man in the world, but at least he had stuck to Jemima's story, and what few things she'd said about it.

Not her personal life. And that was a big, fat, red dividing line between him and professionals like Andrews.

Not that Andrews was the only one. Even Delores would do it, if she could. He took another drag on the cigarette and frowned.

Jemima was watching him with a puzzled expression.

"Why did we drive around and around in circles for so long?" she asked. "Are we lost?"

He glanced at her. "No." He looked out the window, had a brief argument with his conscience, and lost. He turned to her.

"Look, Duchess – you're a very rich person. That's a wonderful thing, but you have to be a little more careful now than you used to be."

She frowned. "What do you mean?"

"I mean, there are people who" – he paused – "might try to take advantage of your good nature. Now that you're rich."

She crossed her arms. "Like who?"

He raised his eyebrows and looked at her ruefully. "Let's just say that I know some of them."

Jemima stared at him again out of those lovely green eyes. "Are you one of them?" she asked.

He winced inside – it was a reasonable question – but he met her gaze.

"No, I am not."

He was gratified to see her blush, and lower her eyes; but he wasn't entirely sure that he'd told her the truth.

"It's your life, and I don't have the right to tell you what to do. I'm just saying that it'd be smart not to make any new friends right now. Because there are going to be lots of people who will want to be your new friends."

Jemima looked troubled. "You mean people will be coming out to our farm." She turned to him. "Like you did."

This time it was his turn to go red, but he nodded. "That's right." He attempted a sickly smile. "But they won't have my sterling qualities – or my charm."

She felt quiet again, and didn't say anything else for more than an hour, during which time he chain-smoked and she sat quietly watching the countryside. The passing landscape slowly melted from skyscrapers, to smaller skyscrapers, to office buildings, to shopping malls, to suburbs, and then to open countryside.

Now and then he stole a glance at her out of the corner of his eye, wondering what she was thinking. It was hard to tell, and even harder to concentrate, because he could never look at her for long without his brains getting scrambled by her beauty. Today, it was the riotous curls of bright coppery hair. Even her severe hairstyle couldn't control them. Little curling wisps escaped all around the edge of her cap, and framed her face more poignantly that any painting. She looked like some Dutch Renaissance masterpiece. She had that dreamy beauty and melting feminine softness.

That could, unfortunately, turn in an instant to Puritanical indignation.

Suddenly, and apropos of nothing recent, she twisted to look at him, and her eyes were stern and unblinking. "You lied to me, Brad Williams. You told me, that you were only going to come out to my house once, and no more, and you came back and back. You said that you weren't going to take my picture, but you took it anyway – with that other man's hands! You told me that you were going to respect my wishes, but you've done just what you wanted to do, from beginning to end!"

Brad nodded dryly. That was the trouble with the Amish –

they didn't understand ethical complexities or completely acceptable shades of gray.

"Now, Duchess—"

"And you call me some name that isn't mine, and why I don't know, because I never invited you to!"

By this time the truck was bouncing along the back roads just minutes from her farm. Rows of shoulder-high corn blocked the view on both sides. Brad felt his heartbeat quickening, and his face going red. He objected: "A friendly nickname. Why all the sturm und drang, Duch– Jemima?"

She was warming to her subject. "It's not a nickname. And when you call me this, it means you have no respect. No respect for what I say, no respect for my home, no respect even for my name!"

Now he was getting a little alarmed. She sounded really angry, and it was important not to let her get him stirred up, too. He put out one hand, as if to reassure her. "Sweetheart, please calm down, now…"

For some reason, those words acted on her like an electric shock. She straightened to her full height, and her eyes blazed.

"I am not your sweetheart," she cried, "I am not your Duchess, I am not a–" she struggled for words – "a doll without a face!"

He could feel his own face going red. He wasn't mad, but yes, he was plenty – something. He told himself that it was important not to get stirred up. But a wave of heat surged through him from the bottom up and made his heart pound in his neck – and scrambled his brain.

Again.

"Why are you making me out the bad guy?" he sputtered. "Hey, I just helped you become the richest girl in the county! I would think I'd earned a little something – if not genuine gratitude, then at least a token thank you!"

She acted as if she hadn't even heard him. To his dismay, she wasn't even looking at him. She was staring out the windshield as if she saw some drooling monster on the other side of it.

"No, and you don't even have respect for me, for my – for my person! You even grabbed me and kissed me, without so much as a handshake or, or a question, much less permission! You're a-a–" she sputtered, and lapsed into angry German again.

He jerked the truck to a stop in front of her house and turned to face her. She already had her fingers on the door handle. In an instant she'd be gone.

He bit his lip. What the heck. If she was this angry with him now, she wasn't going to let him come back, anyway. And he couldn't bear to leave her without even a goodbye.

He grabbed her by the shoulders, looked down into those blazing green eyes for a split-second, and gave her the kiss of his life. It was even crazier and more desperate than the last one, more fiery, more frantic, and more likely to ensure that she'd never speak to him ever again.

But he didn't care.

Mother of mercy, the lips – he'd never met anything like them, they melted like a receding wave into that silky mouth. His heart jumped into his throat.

That mouth that was kissing him back. Yes, yes, yes!

But that delightful moment suddenly came crashing down. The sound of an outraged voice boomed from outside. Brad raised his eyes over Jemima's head, and to his horror, the red-haired giant filled the window behind her. The giant grabbed the door handle, and when he found it locked, he simply ripped the passenger side door right off the truck. It peeled off the hinges with a hideous sound of tearing metal, and Jemima pulled out of his arms and shrieked crazily in German.

Jemima's father reached in and lifted his tiny daughter out of the passenger seat and set her down on the grass. Then he turned back.

Brad grabbed the wheel and gunned the motor, and the truck lurched over the dirt road with a roar. He sent it hurtling towards east Egypt without any clear idea of where he was going, or any real concern. He lifted terrified eyes to the rearview.

The giant was standing in the middle of the road with one hand on his hip, and the other clenched in a fist. He was shaking it.

Brad almost closed his eyes in relief. When he looked down at his hands they were trembling – whether from passion or terror, he couldn't tell. But one thing was for sure. He turned his eyes to the open cavity on the side of the truck. He was going to have a time explaining this to Delores.

CHAPTER NINETEEN

Brad Williams laced his fingers and stared at his computer screen. One last reading before it went to print:

Local Amish girl finds Washington letter worth $1.6 mil

Serenity, PA—Jemima King of Lancaster County was the lucky finder of a letter written by George Washington. Miss King's letter was verified by appraisers as a genuine and previously undiscovered correspondence from Washington to his wife, Martha, probably written during the Revolutionary War. It was recently sold at Brinkley's Auction House in Philadelphia for $1.6 million.

Miss King says she found the letter hidden in the back of an antique clock that she purchased at the Satterwhite Gift Shop in downtown Serenity.

"I didn't know what it was at first," Miss King said. "It was very sweet, a letter from a man in love. You could tell that he was worried that he might not see his wife again.

"I was glad that the letter turned out to be real, and that he got to come back again to Mrs. Washington. I like to think that they were happy."

The director of Brinkley's, William Danforth, says that interest in the letter was intense. "We haven't seen a letter like this for years," he commented. "The rarity of the letter, coupled with the intense interest, combined to push the price past a million dollars – a new high for this type of historical document."

Miss King says that the sale will have no impact on her way of life, and that she plans to save the money.

The anonymous buyer is a collector of American historical documents, and lives in Washington D.C.

Brad frowned, and bit his lip. His first major story in print.

He looked at the photo. It hurt his ego to admit it, but just as he'd suspected, the photo was what made the story. Jemima's beautiful, innocent eyes looked up at the camera like some adorable fawn's. She was such a fantasy girl that it was hard to believe she was really one of the "plain people."

He leaned back into his chair and sighed. He felt like an idiot, and he wouldn't want anyone else to know it, but he'd uploaded the other four photos Eddie had taken onto a thumb drive and meant to keep them, since he wasn't going to see her again.

He closed out the story and opened the photo file.

Eddie had been fast; there he was, giving the Duchess a celebratory hug when the sale figure had been finalized. Her little fingers curled over his back, and she was staring into space, as if she couldn't believe it.

Then, a split-second later, the two of them half-turned toward the camera. The Duchess was now looking stunned and a little scared; and his expression was one of dawning comprehension and anger.

In the third – the one they ran, and cropped to only show Jemima – she was looking full into the camera with that deer-in-the-headlights look.

And the last, a giant hand covering the lens. His hand.

Brad cursed under his breath. Eddie, I'm going to send to Duluth on the principle, you sneaky little weasel!

The sound of his office door opening made him close the file quickly and look up. Delores stood in the opening, hand on hip.

"Well, wonder boy, are you still game?"

He pursed his lips and reached back to open his wallet. He pulled out a bill and slapped it on the desk. "Fifty."

Delores smirked, and set another bill down beside it. "Well, we just went live. It's the moment of truth, hot shot. Let's see if you stay an intern -- or become a *reporter*."

Brad drew a deep breath and clicked over to the Ledger's social media page. There was his story, and that stunning picture of Jemima.

He dropped his eyes to the story's page views, and Delores moved behind his chair to look.

One view. Five, fifteen. Then…nothing.

Brad went very still. He could feel his heart beating in his throat. Come on, come on.

Sixteen views. One share, two. The first comment:

'Wow she's so beautiful!'

Followed by:

'Wow she's so RICH! Marry me, gorgeous!'

Brad exhaled and looked up at Delores. Her face was as unreadable as stone.

Twenty views, twenty-five. Five shares, thirty-five views.

More comments:

'Why don't I ever find anything like this?'

'Hey, I've been to that store!'

Fifty views. Ten shares, sixty, sixty-five views.

Brad glanced at his watch. They'd been live for less than five minutes.

Seventy-nine views, twelve shares. More comments:

'What did the letter say?'

Delores stirred behind him. "Put a link to the Washington letter at the end of your story."

Brad straightened and tapped keys. "There you go." His eyes returned to the page views.

And widened. Damn—just in that short time – two hundred sixty views, fifty-one shares. More comments:

'If I were her, I'd get on a plane and never look back. Aruba, baby!'

'She looks like a painting.'

'Think she'd turn English?'

Three hundred thirty-seven views. Sixty shares.

Delores' secretary walked in, smiling. "The Amish Barbie

story just got picked up by Channel Four."

Brad frowned at her, but Delores only asked: "Did they credit us?"

"Yeah."

Delores relaxed and turned to look at Brad. "Well, it looks like you earned your wings, wonder boy. You were right. It's going to be big."

She placed a large hand on his shoulder. "You're now a full-time reporter for the Ledger. You just earned fifty dollars. And lunch, on me. I'm taking the office to O'Malley's to celebrate."

Brad looked up at her in relief and tried to smile, but his mouth wasn't working right. His lips felt like they were crooked.

"We'll talk about your salary and your new assignments tomorrow. No more yokum stories for you, my boy! Get your coat," Delores commanded, and swept out of the room like a ship casting off to sea.

The pretty secretary lingered and Brad noticed, with surprise, that she had a distinct gleam in her eye. She slid one hip over the edge of his desk and swung a shapely leg in his direction. "Looks like you've scored big. Congratulations, Brad."

He met her eyes. They were large and blue. One of them

winked at him.

He smiled faintly, and then turned his lips down. Oh, why not. It might be good for him to get the Duchess out of his system. Or, at least try.

He picked up his coat and slung it over one shoulder, and extended an arm to the giggling blonde girl. "You're coming with us to O'Malley's, right?" he asked.

"Sure," she purred, and took his arm.

But after they had walked out, the comments continued to appear on the social media page.

'I'm in love!'

'She must be wearing makeup. Nobody looks that good naturally!'

'I bet the house where she lives is picturesque. I wish I could see it!'

CHAPTER TWENTY

Jemima looked up into her father's face fearfully. His expression reminded her of a huge, dark thunderhead just before a cloudburst.

"Daed–"

"Silence!" he barked, and she closed her mouth and looked down at her shoes.

They were standing out on the front lawn; he, with his massive arms crossed, and she, wishing she could make herself invisible. The mangled truck door was lying on the ground, just as it had fallen when her father had pulled it off of Brad William's truck.

Her father took a deep breath, and seemingly, got a new grip on his patience. "Now, Jemima," he said evenly, "we are going inside, and you are going to explain to your mother, and to me, why you did not go to your aunt's, as you told us. And where you were all day. And why you came back here in the company of an Englisch reporter." His voice gathered bass undertones, like a giant organ. "And why–"

Jemima raised her eyes. There were tears in them, and her lips were quivering. "Oh, Daed," she cried, "I'm sorry! But you don't understand! It was the will of God!"

He raised his brows, and tilted his head slightly, as if he mistrusted his ears.

"Oh, yes – if you'll only let me explain!" Jemima cried earnestly.

"You'll have plenty of chance to do that, young lady," he promised her grimly, and took her arm. He marched her up the front steps, and across the porch, and into the house. The screen door slammed behind them.

"Rachel!" he called. "Come and see what your daughter has done!"

Rachel King came down the stairs, her face a question mark. Jemima burst into tears, her mother held out her arms, and she went into them, sobbing.

Rachel met her husband's eyes over Jemima's head.

Her husband responded as if he had been severely rebuked. "Now, Rachel, it's no use to give me that look. You don't know what's just happened!"

"I know that our daughter is in tears, Jacob," she replied softly, looking down at Jemima's face. "What did you say to her?"

Her husband looked wounded. "Me? I am upholding standards in this house. Our daughter did not go to her aunt's house, as she told us. She has been somewhere else, all day long. I walked out into the yard just now to see her in the arms of a strange boy – an Englisch reporter!"

Rachel pulled back from her daughter and stared up into her face. "Jemima, is that true?"

Jemima nodded, and burst out into fresh tears.

Rachel looked at her husband again, and this time her eyes held worry. "Come, sit down at the table, Jemima," she said, and put an arm around her. "You can tell us what happened. We aren't angry, are we, Jacob?"

Her husband rolled his eyes, and threw up his hands, but followed her without objection.

Rachel helped Jemima into a chair, and then took one beside her. "Now, Jemima, tell us what happened," she urged.

Jemima sobbed into her apron. "When, when I went to the store a few months ago," she gulped, "and bought the little clock for Deborah, I found a piece of paper in it," she stuttered. "It was a l-letter."

"The letter you showed me?" her father interjected.

Jemima nodded. "Two Englischers came here to ask me about the letter. One of them wanted to buy it, and the other was the reporter." She was shaken by another gust of tears.

"It was a letter from George Washington. The reporter said it was worth a lot of money, and I should have someone look at it."

"And you gave it to him?" her mother asked.

Jemima looked up at her, her beautiful eyes swimming. "I tried to give it to the reporter," she whispered, "but he gave it back, and said he had showed it to the appraisers, and that it was worth a fortune!"

Rachel looked quickly at her husband, and he leaned close.

"Jemima – are you telling us that you – that you sold the letter?"

Jemima nodded, and burst out into guilty sobs.

Her parents looked at each other. Jacob leaned back in his chair, dumbfounded, and Rachel looked down at the table in stunned silence before recovering.

"Was that why you were with the Englischer?"

Jemima nodded. "He took me to the auction house today,"

she sniffed, and wiped her eyes. "I watched the people bidding on it, and they just wouldn't stop. They went on and on, until the letter sold." She looked up at her mother woefully.

"One million six hundred thousand dollars!" she whispered.

Jacob King burst out into startled German, and his wife covered her mouth with one hand. Their eyes met over Jemima's head.

There was a long, pregnant silence. Jacob took a deep breath and went on, slowly: "You still haven't explained, Jemima King, why I saw you with the Englischer, doing what no good Amish girl should do with a boy she doesn't know?"

Jemima's lips trembled. "It was just – he – was so understanding," she stammered, "and so helpful, and he didn't take the letter for himself when he could have, that I–"

Jacob nodded grimly. "Ha! An Englischer trick, to gain your trust! What did I tell you, Jemima, when you first found the letter? You would have done better to listen. Now, we must go to the bishop with this news of the letter, and see what he will say."

His eye returned to his errant daughter. "And why did you tell me it was the will of God?" he asked.

Jemima shook her head. "The Sunday after I got the news

that the letter was worth so much, the preacher said, What if a miracle happened? What if I had a million dollars and kept it back from the poor? And I thought that God was speaking to me. And that He meant me to sell this letter. And to give the money to help the people who need it, like Adam Yoder, and his parents."

Jemima's mother reached for her, and took her into her arms. She looked at her husband through swimming eyes, and kissed her daughter's hair. "There, you see Jacob, her heart was right. I think that was a fine thing to do, Jemima. You're not in trouble. Everything will be all right, you'll see. Now go up to your bedroom, and wash, and get ready for bed."

Jemima sniffed, and dried her eyes, and looked up gratefully at her mother, and timidly at her father, and retreated.

After she had gone, Jacob crossed his arms and looked at his wife ruefully. "What good does it do for me to try to have discipline in this house, Rachel, when you pet our children so?"

His wife looked at him affectionately. "I know you, Jacob King," she smiled serenely. "You feel the same as I do, and you're right to try to keep them safe. But Jemima did no wrong."

"No wrong? You didn't see her, she was kissing that Englischer as if he was the last young man on earth. I don't know who he is, but it's plain he has designs on her – and the money he thinks he can get out of her! I don't want Jemima's life to be ruined and her heart broken, by some–"

His wife shook her head. "But Jacob, it's her rumspringa. It isn't good, I know, but if we make too big a fuss, we make it into something bigger than it is, maybe. Jemima has three healthy young Amish boys who are in love with her. One of them will make her forget this Englisch boy, you'll see."

"Well–"

"And the money, Jacob," his wife insisted, leaning toward him – "we must tell the bishop, yes, but Jemima hasn't joined the church yet, and she isn't bound to do what we would. The money is hers, Jacob. We can't force her to do anything with it."

Her husband looked at her grimly. "She's a 17-year-old girl, Rachel. She doesn't understand how to deal with money wisely. Do you want to see your daughter in Englisch clothes, and wearing makeup, or buying a television – or a car?"

His wife frowned, and shook her head. "No, Jacob," she replied simply. "But we must trust her, and trust God. He will help her to do the right thing."

Her husband's expression softened and he threw up his hands. "This is why I never win an argument with you, my Rachel," he sighed, and then leaned over and kissed her ruefully.

CHAPTER TWENTY-ONE

The next morning found Jemima out in the back yard of her parent's home, hanging clothes on the clothesline. It was still early; there was mist still hovering in the low folds of the hills, and the air was still pleasantly cool.

Jemima picked up a wet dress and draped it over the clothesline. Breakfast had been subdued and mostly silent. Her parents had said nothing about her embarrassing predicament. She wasn't sure if Deborah knew what had happened, because she, too, had been silent.

Jemima frowned, wondering why Deborah hadn't told their parents about seeing her walk off into the bushes with a stranger. But to be honest, she wasn't really worried about it –

just grateful.

She had other and much bigger things to be worried about.

It was only a matter of time now before someone saw the story in the newspaper, and the word got out in the community that Jemima King was a rich millionaire. She wondered if people would think that she was greedy for money and full of hochmut. She wondered what they would make of the fact that she'd talked to an Englisch reporter, and had gone all the way to the city with him, alone.

Or, more specifically – what Mark and Samuel and Joseph would make of it.

She shook her head, and stamped her foot and cried. It was that Englischer reporter – if he hadn't done what he'd promised not to do, if he hadn't grabbed her and kissed her again, she would've had time to get inside before her father caught them, and at least she could've had a few days of privacy before everyone found out. But now, even that was gone.

She grabbed up another dress and slapped it over the line savagely. Brad Williams was a liar. He had done only what he had wanted to do; he had no concern for anyone but himself.

And the thing that upset her most was that she was never going to see him again.

The sudden sound of her father's voice brought her sharply back to the present. His voice was raised in outrage and – yes – it was unmistakably anger.

It was coming from the front porch.

Jemima dropped a shirt onto the grass and ran around the side of the house. She was just in time to see a white truck scratch off down the road in a cloud of dust. She looked up at her father.

He was watching the truck as it left, and muttering in what her mother sometimes called "Low German."

When he turned back, and saw her standing there, he put his hands on his hips and regarded her with awful irony.

"So, here you are, hoping to see that hound again? No, my addled daughter, it wasn't him!" he said tartly. "It was a man from another such Englischer rag, full of questions about things that are none of his business! Now go back to your chores, and pray to God to be healed of silliness in the head!"

He relapsed into ominous muttering, and Jemima turned her eyes to the road. The truck was still visible, a tiny white dot speeding back to the city.

"Oh, Daed," she objected, but he waved her away, and retired to the house in disgust.

Jemima settled back into her chores, and they had quiet for all the rest of that day. But soon after nightfall, when they were all in bed, there was a loud rapping on the front door.

Jemima got up out of bed and went to the window that faced the front yard. There was a van parked outside and several people climbing out of it. Jemima's heartbeat quickened. There was a big "Channel 10" logo painted on the side of the van. For an instant she hoped that Brad Williams would be with them – but no, he worked for a newspaper, not a television station.

One of the strangers lit a giant lamp, and the whole front of the house was suddenly flooded with blinding light. Jemima gasped and closed the curtain.

She could hear her father stomping down the stairs, and pulling on his pants as he went. The door creaked open, and Jemima could clearly hear a woman's voice:

"Hi, I'm Pamela Harrison with Channel 10 News – ah, that's a news station out of Philadelphia – and I was hoping to ask you a few questions about–"

Her usually-civil father cut her off. "We were all in bed, and we have nothing to say to anyone, about anything. Please go away, and leave us alone."

He shut the door with a bang.

But, Jemima was quick to note, he did not come back upstairs.

Voices muttered unintelligibly from below; the strangers seemed to be holding a conference of some kind. Then there was the sound of footsteps on the porch steps. She moved gingerly toward the window again, taking care not to show herself in it.

A group of four people were standing on their lawn in front of the van. Their silhouettes were razor-sharp against the huge light. The woman was very smartly dressed in a pantsuit and heels, but the others – photographers, she guessed – were dressed in oversized shirts, baggy pants, and sneakers.

Suddenly, the woman's voice boomed out over a microphone: "Jemima, we know you live here. We'd like to talk to you. Please call us at Channel 10 News."

Jemima turned her head. Now she could hear her mother's bare feet rushing downstairs, and she knew why: it was to keep her father from bursting out the front door.

She could hear her mother's low, pleading voice downstairs, followed by her father's – the bass organ sound was very strong now – followed by a soft scuffling sound, and her mother's voice again, very urgent.

To Jemima's relief, the painful brightness suddenly died. The intruders packed the lamp up again, and slowly climbed back into the van.

The van's lights flicked on, and the motor growled, and the van slowly rolled away over the long dirt road.

Jemima slumped against her bedroom wall and closed her eyes. Her heart was pounding with a mixture of fright, and deep embarrassment.

Because every other family in the valley had heard the woman's giant voice calling for Jemima King to "come out and talk."

She put her face in her hands and cried. But before long she heard her father's big feet climb the stairs, and then pause outside her door.

It swung open gently, and his tousled head of red hair appeared in the opening.

"Mima, are you all right?"

"Oh, Daed!" she sobbed.

He held out his arms and she went running into them. She wept on his shoulder as he patted her back with one huge hand.

"There now, Mima, my girl," he soothed, "there's no reason to be upset. We all know that Englischers are crazy in the head. They are doing what they do. But soon something new will happen, and they'll forget all about this, and leave us alone. Eh?"

He looked down at her. "Come now, let me see a smile, my brave girl."

Mima swallowed, and looked up into his face, and

mustered a weak smile. A tender light dawned over his face, and he smoothed her hair back.

"That's what I like to see. Now go back to bed, and don't worry. Your father is here, and he won't let anyone bother you."

He gave her a quick peck on the cheek, helped her back into bed, and pulled the covers up around her chin.

Then he smiled down at her reassuringly, walked out of the room, and closed the door softly behind him.

But after he was gone, Jemima bit the sheets with her teeth, and squeezed her eyes together, and wept again. Not entirely from fright, as her father had supposed.

Now she was angry, too.

CHAPTER TWENTY-TWO

The next Sunday, Jemima stood next to her mother and Deborah at worship. It was a beautiful midsummer's morning, a temptation to wandering eyes, but her eyes, and her mother's eyes, and Deborah's eyes, were all glued to the floor of Silas Yoder's barn.

Because that morning, Jacob King was one of the penitents making a public confession of sin.

He stood next to the bishop, hand in hand, head bowed, as the bishop asked him gently:

"What sin do you confess, Brother Jacob?"

Jemima stole a glance at her mother. She had closed her

eyes, and appeared to be praying.

Her father cleared his throat, and intoned: "I confess the sin of anger."

The bishop nodded. "And how did you commit this sin?"

Her father cleared his throat. "I tore the door off of a man's truck."

The bishop looked momentarily startled, and added, faintly: "Was that the only sin you wish to confess?"

Jacob shook his head. "No."

"What other sin do you confess, brother?"

"I brought down a flying camera that was taking pictures of my home. With a rock. And," he coughed, "I chased a couple of men with a shovel, and drove them off of my property."

The bishop nodded. "Is there any more?"

"Yes."

Jemima looked at her mother again. Her eyes were still closed, and she was frowning slightly.

Jacob cast an apologetic glance at his wife. "I – ah, I threw a woman into a pond. And her camera."

The bishop bit his lip, and nodded.

"Are you truly penitent, brother?"

There was a long moment of silence. To Jemima's astonishment, her mother coughed aloud, and Jacob sighed: "Yes, um, yes I am."

"Very well, brother."

Jacob nodded to the bishop, and returned to his seat on the men's benches, and the bishop led the closing prayer.

After the service, Jacob rejoined his family, and Rachel put her hand on his arm in a rare public display of affection. She beamed at him, and he pretended not to notice it, but Jemima noticed that he sometimes looked at her mother out of the corner of his eye, and smiled such a tiny smile, that no one who wasn't looking would've seen it.

But to judge by her smile, Jemima was fairly certain that her mother had seen it.

They sat down at long tables for lunch out under the sky, the eldest first, as always, and Jemima busied herself helping. But she was shy and didn't try to meet her neighbor's eyes, because this was the first Sunday since her embarrassing problem had become common knowledge, and she was nervous.

No one had been unkind; in fact, many of them spoke to her in what sounded like sympathetic tones, but she knew without having to ask that everyone knew everything.

Because her new fame had become a problem for the whole community.

The bishop and a group of elders had been obliged to go to local government and request a police presence in the first frantic week after the story became public because it had generated not just local, but national interest. All kinds of people were streaming to the area uninvited: the press first, followed by the rest of the world – tourists, the curious, men who claimed to be in love with her, people who wanted her to give money to their cause (or to them) and even those who were plainly mentally ill.

Deborah had been scared out of her wits by a man who had appeared out of one of their haystacks like a ghost; but she had been so outraged, and had given him such a fierce tongue lashing, that he had run away.

One of Jemima's geese had been stolen from its pen, and had later appeared on an online auction site advertised as "The million-dollar Amish goose." It had reportedly sold for five times its true value, and had acquired its own web site on the Internet, where, she had heard, thousands of people visited every day to see the goose wear funny hats, and ride a skateboard.

Her own mother had even been accosted in their backyard by a woman with a camera who shot video of her without her permission, until her father had arrived.

And that had resulted in this morning's confession. Jemima

thought, with a pang, that there were probably more confessions to come for her poor father, because there was no sign of the frenzy slowing down, much less stopping. Her father had been forced to barricade the driveway to keep cars and trucks from rolling right up to their door, and he hadn't had time for his work, because it had become necessary to guard the property from intruders all day long, and all night, too.

But what was just as bad, at least in Jemima's mind, was that she hadn't heard a word from any of her suitors since the scandal broke. It was odd and not like them at all, for all three of them to neglect her for a whole week.

She had seen no sign of any of them so far that morning. But when it was her own turn to sit down at the table, she saw with gratitude that at least her friend Ruth Yoder was the same. She came and sat down beside her at the table, and scooted over so that she could giggle and whisper to Jemima about the boys they saw.

And to Jemima's intense relief, Ruth didn't ask her lurid questions about her money, or about the handsome Englischer reporter, or about the circus that had rolled over the entire countryside for the last seven days.

She just sat there, munching jam and bread, and giggling, and pointing out the cute boys, just like always. And at first, that was a tremendous comfort.

Until Jemima noticed that Mark Christner, Samuel Kauffman and Joseph Beiler were, in fact, in attendance that morning.

They just weren't attending her.

Jemima's mouth dropped open in amazement. All three of them – all three – had abandoned her for Miriam Zook.

It wasn't possible!

But she couldn't deny what was right in front of her eyes – there they were, clustered around another girl like bees around a hive of honey. Mark was offering Miriam a bite of his toast, and Samuel was laughing at something she had said, and even poor, shy Joseph was staring up at her with his big calf eyes.

Of course, Miriam was a beauty with her white-blonde hair and coffee-brown eyes, and she was a sweet girl. Jemima set her lips, and made herself admit it: Yes, Miriam was a – a very sweet girl.

But a pang of something so like jealousy stung her, that she was forced to admit that she didn't much care if Miriam Zook's righteousness floated her all the way up to heaven, like a big blonde balloon.

Ruth caught sight of these sad defections an instant later, and she leaned close to whisper, not unkindly: "Close your mouth, Mima! And don't stare. You don't want them to think that you care what they do."

Jemima closed her mouth then, and trained her eyes on her plate. But the rest of the day was ruined for her, and she was intensely conscious that she was now an object of pity as well as of wonder, because she feared that all the teenage girls there, and probably their mothers too, were shaking their heads and saying sadly:

"Poor Jemima King! It turns out that all the money in the world can't buy you love."

CHAPTER TWENTY-THREE

That night, Jemima curled up in a little ball in her favorite chair. It was her Daed's big stuffed chair, the one she had always crawled up into as a child when she wanted to sit on his lap. It was a deep, satisfying, oxblood red, and soft as a dream. And it had that comforting Daed scent of pipe tobacco, and a whiff of fire and steel.

The chair was in his little study, a room that he went to sometimes, all by himself. The chair faced a big stone fireplace, and in the winter, it was the coziest place in the house.

It was too warm for a fire in the middle of summer, but the idea of a fire appealed to Jemima that night. She hugged herself unhappily.

The door creaked open slowly, and when Jemima looked up, her Daed was standing there, looking at her sympathetically. He walked over, pulled up a chair, and crossed his arms over its back. He looked a question.

Jemima looked at him. "Did you mean it, Daed?" she asked quietly.

He raised his eyebrows. "Mean what, Mima?"

"Did you mean it today, when you said you were sorry?" she asked softly, and turned her eyes on his face.

He looked back toward the doorway, and seeing it empty, turned back and replied: "Mima, there are some things we must do if we feel them, or not."

"So you aren't sorry for those things you did?"

"I didn't say that." He looked up at her face briefly. "If you ask me, do I feel sorry, then no; I feel angry. But I know in my mind that anger is wrong, and we must all repent for wrong things."

Jemima digested this. "If it all happened again, would you do things the same?" she asked.

He looked at her, and set his jaw slightly. "I don't know."

"Because I feel angry, too, Daed," she whispered. "So angry! Angry at the Englischer reporter for lying to me, and for being selfish. Angry that he hasn't come back. Angry at the other Englischers for all coming here at once and making us trapped in our own house." She felt tears burn her eyelids, and looked away. "Angry at Mark and Samuel and even Joseph for going after Miriam Zook, and leaving me alone."

Her father's big hand appeared and gently turned her chin to face him. His eyes were sad and sympathetic.

"My poor Mima," he said quietly. "This is your first taste of trouble, my girl! But it won't last for long, you'll see."

"You should have seen them, Daed," she complained, "mooning over Miriam Zook as if she was the only girl on earth, and feeding her things, and laughing like she was so funny, and staring at her like she'd dropped down from the sky. It was horrible to watch!"

Her father's expression had taken on a tinge of amusement. "I did watch it, Mima."

Jemima looked at her father in surprise. "You noticed?"

"Of course I did," he replied. "And do you know what I saw?"

She shook her head.

"I saw three young pups with very bruised feelings, sending a message to a certain young lady. And do you know what that message was?"

Jemima pinched her lips together, and looked away.

"The message was, 'Two can play that game.' Or in your case, my poor Mima – three."

Jemima stared steadfastly out the window, frowning.

"Think of how you'd feel, Mima, if you saw that Mark Christner had gone from courting you one day, to running off to the city with a beautiful Englisch woman, the next."

"It wasn't like that at all!"

"Or that Samuel Kauffman had found something as big as a letter from George Washington, and that he didn't share the news with you. When you thought that you were important to him."

Jemima felt the tears coming back, and frowned.

"Or that Joseph Beiler had suddenly become rich. So rich, that now you were afraid to come near him, because he might misunderstand."

"Oh, Daed –" Jemima whimpered, and looked up into his face "–do you really think so? I never thought of how what I did – how all of this – must have made them feel."

Her father gave her a contemplative peck on the brow, and sighed. "That play-acting with Miriam Zook may have been silly, Mima, but it was a real warning, just the same. Those boys are telling you that you can't take them for granted."

He looked down at her face. "If I were one of them, I wouldn't let you do it, either. You've gotten used to being the queen bee around here, Mima. Maybe you've gotten a little too used to it."

Her father took her into his arms. "Maybe you should stop to think about their feelings, before you make another big decision. At least, you should, if you want one of those pups for a husband."

He sighed, and his big blue eyes looked rueful. "Though it would make things easier for everyone, if you could figure out which one of them you wanted."

Jemima put her arms around her father and frowned. He was right: what she had felt earlier was jealousy, pure and simple. And you couldn't be jealous over someone you didn't love.

She hugged her father closer, and closed her eyes. He had been right about something else, as well. She had been playing fast and loose with something very precious to her: the love of her friends. Mark and Samuel and Joseph were at least that, if not much more, and it had been wrong of her to shut them out.

She looked up at her father. "Do I need to repent, too, Daed?" she whispered.

Her father considered. "Maybe a little, Mima," he said, smiling. "But young men are always very forgiving of a pretty girl. And if they love her – well, she'll hardly have the words out of her mouth, before all is right again."

Jemima smiled, and snuggled back into his chest. "I love you, Daed," she murmured, and closed her eyes.

He rested his cheek on hers. "And I you, little girl."

CHAPTER TWENTY-FOUR

The media frenzy took more than two weeks to calm down enough for Jemima to be able to go out in public without fear of being mobbed; and only then because the local police had begun to jail trespassers and repeat harassers.

But little by little, Jemima began to take small excursions to places besides worship; to her friend's houses mostly, because she still wasn't bold enough to attempt to make her doll deliveries in town. And she wasn't sure she had the heart to do it, anyway. She'd been told by her friends that some of the shops were selling red-haired "Jemima" dolls to the tourists, and that they were outselling even traditional Amish dolls.

Jemima watched the countryside zoom past as their car rolled down the road. The last month had been a nightmare, but the money from Brinkley's had finally arrived in her bank account. Now that she was able, Jemima was determined to make at least one good thing come out of all this mess: she was going to the hospital to tell Adam Yoder's parents that they didn't have to worry about his medical bill.

Her father had asked Mr. Biggams, one of their Englisch neighbors, to drive them to the hospital in his car. Mr. Biggams was one of the few Englischers that her father trusted; he was a kind man, a hard worker, and minded his own business – three traits that her father very much admired.

He was also sympathetic. Jemima noticed that he was careful to take the back roads for as long as possible, and to Jemima's relief, the only other traffic that they saw was their neighbors' buggies.

Jemima was hopeful that she and her father would be able to get to Adam's room unnoticed. Mr. Biggams had warned them against using the main entrance to the hospital, and had promised that he knew a back entrance, closer to the elevators, that would give them privacy.

Her father shared the back seat of the car with her, and occupied four-fifths of it. He filled the space so completely that the girl at the parking lot tollbooth couldn't have seen Jemima if she'd tried, and when Mr. Biggams parked the car right next to a small door, and they all hurried through it,

Jacob King was a more effective shield for his daughter than a cloak of invisibility.

The way that Mr. Biggams knew seemed to be one that visitors weren't meant to use, but the best possible one for their purposes. It wound through a narrow maze of labs, small offices, and examination rooms, most of them empty. The few people they saw were nurses or techs, and all of them were too busy to take notice, and unlikely to ask questions if they did.

Mr. Biggams' indoor trail led at last through a pair of double doors that faced a small elevator. To Jemima's relief, it was already open, and empty, and they hurried in.

"What floor is he on?" Mr. Biggams asked, adjusting his glasses.

"The fourth," her father replied, and their neighbor pushed the button.

When they arrived on the fourth floor, it, too, was relatively empty and quiet. They made it to Adam Yoder's room without notice or comment.

Jacob King knocked softly on the door, and a voice from inside said: "Come in."

Mr. Biggams tactfully declined to enter, and remained outside, but Jemima and her father walked in.

When they entered, Jemima's eyes were drawn like a

magnet to Adam Yoder. The little blond boy was hardly recognizable because most of him was inside a body cast. One arm and two legs were lifted by slings.

His parents were sitting by his bedside, and looked to Jemima as if they hadn't slept in days.

Adam's father, Benjamin, stood up and extended his hand to her father. "Hello, Jacob," he said earnestly, and nodded to Jemima. "Thank you for coming."

Adam's mother, Hannah, smiled at Jemima, and she smiled back, trying not to show the pity that she felt. Her heart went out to them suddenly. It must be awful to be going through such a crisis. She was suddenly ashamed of her own self-pity; her own troubles were nothing in comparison.

"Won't you sit down?" Benjamin asked, but Jacob shook his head.

"We won't stay long. But we wanted to come by and see Adam, and to pray with you. Jemima also wanted to tell you something."

He turned toward her.

Jemima felt her face going red, but she looked full into Benjamin Yoder's face and set her mouth. "I guess you heard about what happened to me," she said steadily. "I just wanted to say that – whatever your hospital bills are, I will pay them. Because, I want to. And I can."

Hannah Yoder burst into tears and covered her mouth with her hand. Benjamin Yoder's eyes moved incredulously from her face to her father's. Jacob nodded.

He shook his head. "I don't – I don't know what to say."

Jacob shook his head. "There's no need to say anything." He looked back at his daughter's face and smiled.

And Jemima allowed herself to smile back. She hadn't expected to feel such pleasure, but she did. In fact, she hadn't felt such pleasure in a long time. She literally felt – warm.

"God bless you," Benjamin said softly, "Jemima King!"

On the way home, Jemima noticed that her father kept looking at her. He didn't say anything, but he was wearing that expression that always meant that he was secretly pleased. No one outside his family would have recognized it – it was too subtle – a certain tilt of his jaw, and the way his eyebrows rode high over his brow.

Jemima looked down and suppressed a smile. Because these were unmistakable signs.

Her father was proud of her.

CHAPTER TWENTY-FIVE

When they got back to the house, Jemima went upstairs to her own bedroom and closed the door behind her. She walked over to the window that looked out over the garden.

The afterglow of her father's approval still lingered; it was like the feeling she had when she had been out in the sun for an hour or two.

She looked up into the fluffy white clouds floating over the fields. Or, maybe, she was feeling something more than just her father's approval. She smiled to herself.

There was so much else she could do, besides just helping the Yoders: she could give money to her parents, so they could have something in case of an emergency. And she had always meant to give a good bit of the money to the community fund, to be used for neighbors in need.

She was still thinking about it, when voices from downstairs interrupted her train of thought. They were coming through the open window – the window directly over the front porch.

She could hear the porch swing groan and creak. Her father's voice called out: "Well! Good afternoon, Mark Christner! We haven't seen you in a while!"

Jemima's heart jumped into her mouth. Her first reaction was joy: her second, was to bite her lip. Her Daed was reminding Mark of his defection, and she was sure that Mark would take his point.

"Good afternoon," Mark's voice replied. His voice definitely had a chastened sound. "Is Jemima home?"

The swing groaned again, as if her father had crossed his legs. "She was here, but the other fellow came by a few minutes ago, and they went for a walk. I couldn't say when they'll be back."

Jemima opened her mouth in shock. How could he?

Then she giggled.

Mark's voice had an edge now. "The other fellow?"

Her father blew his nose, and sniffed. "Yes, the blond one,

I think. There are so many nowadays, I can't keep 'em straight."

Mark's voice was now hard with suspicion. "The blond one! You mean Samuel Kauffman?"

Her father's tone was lazy and nonchalant. "Or, maybe, the boy from Marietta. A guest of her aunt's, they've really hit it off." He coughed. "Shall I give her a message?"

"No. I mean, yes, if you would. Just tell her that I – I came by."

"I'll do that, Mark. Say hello to your folks for me."

Jemima crept to the window and looked down over the porch roof. Soon she could see Mark's black head, followed by his body, walking down the driveway, and out along the road.

He reminded her of nothing so much, as a rooster who'd just lost a fight.

Later that afternoon, she was sitting in that same swing, helping her mother shell beans. Deborah had been commanded to go to the mailbox. She returned and tossed one of the envelopes into Jemima's lap with a grimace.

"Well, he's back," was her disgusted assessment.

Jemima opened the envelope, and three pages of handwritten poetry came tumbling out into her lap. She smiled, well pleased. Joseph was so sweet. He hadn't deserted her, after all!

She picked up the letter and read:

I know that you have fled away from me, for a little while, like a mare that jumps the fence and runs away. But now you have come back to your true pasture.

Her smile faded into a puzzled frown.

You were tempted away by a deceiver with an apple, and have chewed the fruit of the world. It tastes like honey in the mouth, but is bitter in the entrails.

Jemima's frown deepened.

But now you are returned, to a good and pleasant land, with green fields and an abundance of hay.

Jemima's mother was watching her face. "Is something wrong, Jemima?"

She looked up at her mother and hurriedly folded the letter. "Oh – no, no." She tried to smile. "It's from Joseph."

"Good," her mother replied, approvingly.

The next day, just after lunch, the last wanderer returned to the fold. Jemima was in the garden again, picking tomatoes, when two hands went over her eyes. She jumped and shrieked, but Samuel Kauffman's laughter put her instantly at ease.

She turned to face him. "Samuel! You scared me to death!"

He laughed at her, and then went quiet, and pulled a little tendril of hair out from underneath her cap. "Then we're even, Mima," he said softly.

Jemima looked down at the ground, and he took her hand. "Why didn't you tell me about all of it, Mima?" he asked. "I would have understood."

She lifted pleading eyes to his face. "Oh, Samuel, I wanted to, but I was – I was scared. Nothing like it had ever happened to anyone, and I didn't know what to do."

He twirled her hair between his fingers. "And the Englischer – he told you what to do."

Jemima nodded, and looked down again.

She could tell that he tried, but Samuel couldn't keep a tinge of jealousy out of his voice. "Don't let yourself get fooled, Mima. An Englischer man will take advantage of a girl like you. They are out in the world, they have no honor."

Jemima looked up at him gratefully. "You're very sweet to be worried about me, Samuel," she told him.

He took her in his arms. "I can't help it," he smiled. "I care about you."

He was going to tell her he loved her. Jemima gasped and searched Samuel's eyes. They held hers steadily – but to her disappointment, he said no more.

She smiled and hugged him anyway. After the awful month she had endured, she had learned a painful but valuable lesson. Namely, that it was wisest to be happy with what you had, instead of reaching for what you didn't.

All three of her suitors were back in the fold, and she didn't intend to do anything to drive them out again.

At least, not until she knew which one of them was her husband.

CHAPTER TWENTY-SIX

Mark Christner returned to the house two days later, and this time her father gave him admittance. Jemima had to cover a smile, to see what a timid return Mark made. He was normally so self-confident!

"Mima, may I see you outside?" he asked humbly.

Jemima smiled and nodded, and he led her out past the front porch, out across the lawn, and down to the edge of a little pond that fronted the road. There was a willow tree there, and a swing, and they sat down in it.

Mark looked out over the water a long time, and Jemima felt sorry for him. Words had never been Mark's strong suit, and she could see that he was struggling with them now. Finally he turned to her, with those beautiful blue eyes, ringed by dark lashes. And just said:

"What happened, Mima?"

For some reason, the way he said it went through her like a spear. Jemima felt tears in her eyes, and shook her head.

"It was too big for me, that's all, Mark," she murmured. "It got out of hand so fast. I met the Englischer reporter at Mr. Satterwhite's store when I bought the clock. He bumped into me, and the letter popped out of the back, so he saw it. And he saw another man wanting to the buy the clock very badly. I guess he just – guessed that the letter might be worth money.

"And they both came to the house and were arguing. And the reporter kept shouting that the letter was worth money. And it all got so confusing that I-I just mailed the letter to the reporter, Mark. I just wanted it to go away."

She raised troubled eyes to his. "But what was strange, Mark, was that – he didn't take it. The Englischer reporter didn't take the letter, or the money. He wrote me back, and told me he'd had it appraised, and that they were holding it for me. He promised to help me sell it."

She looked down at her hands again. "If only I would – let them write a story about it."

Mark was frowning, looking out at the horizon as if he saw it on fire. He nodded. "I can see what happened, Mima," he said angrily. "The Englischer was using you."

He turned to her, and added earnestly: "There's more than one kind of greed, Mima. You can be greedy for fame as much as for money. And some people are. They're sick with hochmut." He shook his head solemnly. "The Englischer used you, Mima."

Jemima felt her lower lip trembling – because she knew he was right. Mark had always had more common sense than most people, and he was right. He had seen instantly what she was only just realizing.

The reporter had used her.

Mark's eyes took on a sympathetic look. "I hope he didn't hurt you, Mima."

Jemima looked up at him, and smiled, and shook her head. "Oh, no!" she said stoutly, "the idea! It's true that he – liked to flirt, but it was very plain that he did that all the time, with every girl he met. Oh, no," she assured him. "I wasn't hurt."

And, she thought to herself, it was true. She wasn't hurt, at least not anymore. She was angry.

Mark relaxed visibly. He seemed to exhale.

"I'm glad," he said simply. "I hate to think of you being hurt, Mima." He reached out and twined his brown fingers in hers.

He looked at her again. "What are you going to do now?"

She met his eyes unhappily. "I don't know," she moaned. "I let the Englischer talk me into selling the letter, because I prayed to God, and I thought He was telling me to give the money to people who needed it. So, I am. Doing that, I mean."

Mark looked at her affectionately. "I figured you would." He put her hand to his lips. "You've always had a big heart."

His smile faded, and he looked down at the ground. "But until you finish, it gives me a problem, Mima."

She looked a question, but he didn't meet her eyes. "I can't court with a millionaire," he blurted.

He looked up again. "Mima, you know how I feel, but I can't. I won't have people saying, that Mark Christner is tagging after Mima King for her money. I won't do it."

Jemima sucked in her breath. Her Daed had been right. She raised her eyebrows, and sputtered: "B-but, Mark, it wouldn't make any difference. Nothing has changed. I haven't changed."

Mark's eyes took on a keen look, almost like pain. He shook his head. "Yes, you have, Mima. You used to be a beautiful girl. Now, you're a beautiful millionaire."

Jemima looked down at the ground, and shrugged painfully. "But I just told you, that – that I never meant to keep it. I mean to give the money away."

Mark squeezed her hand. "I know, Mima. Tell me when you're done." He leaned over to kiss her, and then got up and walked away.

Jemima sat staring at the water for a long time after. She felt as if someone had punched her in the stomach, but Mark hadn't meant to be cruel. Just the opposite – Mark was just trying to be honest, to let her know that he wasn't after her for her money. It was noble, and admirable, and good.

And she bowed her head, and cried bitterly over it for well over an hour. Because she knew now that it was only a matter of time before she had this conversation again with Samuel, and even with Joseph. They were Amish boys, they'd been raised right, and they would never let anyone think they weren't honest.

Especially when it came to love.

After a while her father came down to the lake and settled down in the swing beside her. He put his big arm around her shoulder and let her rest her head on his chest.

Her father looked up at the sky. "He told you he wasn't going to court with a rich girl, didn't he, Mima?"

Jemima nodded, and cried: "Why didn't you tell me, Daed?"

He leaned down and kissed her. "Would that have made it any easier?"

She sniffed, and shook her head.

"No. Well, Mima, you're just going to have to choose. No decent boy will let people think he wants a girl for her money. None of your pups is going to stand for that, at least, not if he's worth having. I'm glad that at least one of them proved that he is worth having."

"Oh Daed," she replied indignantly, "Samuel and Joseph are too, and you know it!"

He chuckled. "Do I? I suppose. But let them prove it. You know, Mima, all of this may have a silver lining after all. It will show you which of those boys mean business about you, and which love you just for yourself."

Jemima buried her face in his shirt and nodded. "Maybe so, Daed," she mourned, "but right now, it just feels awful."

"I know," he soothed, and patted her shoulder. "Come inside, my girl, and stop moping out here. We're in sight of the road. You don't want to be in the papers again, do you?"

"Oh, Daed!" she cried, but then sputtered out a little laugh.

Her father looked down at her tenderly. "That's what I like to see. You're going to be all right, Mima – I promise. Come."

Jemima took her father's hand, and let him lead her back

up the hill to the house. But she set her mouth into a hard, thin line. There was only one question in her mind:

What was the world's fastest time, for giving away a million dollars?

Because she was about to beat the record.

THE END

Thank you for Reading!

And thank you for supporting me as an independent author! I hope you enjoyed reading this book as much as I loved writing it!

In the next chapter, there is a FREE sample of the next book in the series, An Amish Country Treasure 3. You can find it at your favorite online booksellers in eBook and Paperback format.

All the Best

Ruth

AN AMISH COUNTRY TREASURE 3

Faced with a lawsuit and torn between four anxious suitors -- one an Englischer who has already once betrayed her trust -- will Jemima King find the strength to stand for herself and her family? Or will greed and mistrust steal away everything she values?

After resolving to give away her fortune, Amish teen Jemima King's problems are far from over. She faces a million dollar lawsuit and a heartwrenching decision between three Amish suitors and the Englisch reporter who -- in spite of his betrayal -- still has fingerholds on her heart. Will Jemima find the strength to make the right choices? Or will this Amish treasure spell the destruction of her family and future?

CHAPTER ONE

"But *Daed*!"

Jemima King's lovely green eyes pled with her father's implacable blue ones, but when it came to a battle of wills, it was no contest. The head of the house sputtered an incredulous whoof, as if he couldn't believe what he'd just heard, and Jemima quickly lowered her eyes in defeat.

But Jemima's mother dimpled, and reached out to caress her oldest daughter's cheek. "Your father said no, and no it is," she told Jemima. "But it was very sweet of you to offer. It shows that your heart is in the right place." Rachel met her husband's gaze, and a look of approval passed between them.

Then Jacob raised his table napkin and wiped his mouth – a signal that the discussion was over.

"Well, that's that! Are we ready to go?" He trained his bright eyes on Jemima's face.

She looked up at him pleadingly and made one last try. "But Daed! It doesn't make sense for me to give that much money to the Yoders', and none to my own –"

Her father's answer was to slap his hands on his knees,

stand up suddenly, and announce to the room at large: "Well, I'm going now! Everyone who wants to come with me had better shake a leg."

He made good on his threat immediately; he strode across the living room, opened the front door, and walked out.

Jemima's mother turned to her with a smile. "He's proud of you," she said softly and put her coffee cup to her lips. "And so am I."

Jemima met her eyes unhappily. "I may not be all that good. I want to give the money away, at least partly so I can see Mark and Samuel and Joseph again! All of them told me that they couldn't court with me anymore. Or at least, not while I'm so rich." She sighed, and kicked one of the table legs with a small foot.

Her mother reached for her hand. "Well, after today, everything will be back to normal," she reassured her. "When you give the money to the community fund, all of this will be behind you, and your – your admirers will be back over here every day, giving your father headaches."

Her mother laughed, and Jemima finally broke down and joined in. It was such a wonderful thought that she couldn't help dwelling on it – the prospect of getting this Englisch letter business over for good.

And getting her young men back!

She took one last sip of coffee and patted her lips with a napkin. "I guess I need to go," she sighed. "The sooner I begin, the sooner it'll be done!"

Jemima followed her father across the living room, and out the front door. She paused on the porch steps, and breathed in the cool morning air, and let her eyes wander over the vista.

It was overcast: low, heavy clouds scudded over the green fields and veiled the hills. The mild breeze was fragrant of rain. It was pleasantly cool, a reminder that fall wasn't far away.

But another, less pleasant sight met Jemima's eyes too: one that she hadn't expected. Instead of her father waiting patiently for her in the buggy, he was standing beside Rufus, hands on hips. He was staring at a line of cars, parked by the side of the road, about 300 yards away.

Roughly a stone's throw away.

The strangers were smart to keep their distance, Jemima thought grimly. While the trespassers had never respected her family's privacy, they'd quickly learned to respect the fact that her father was a good shot with a rock.

Jemima pinched her lips into a straight line. She could tell at once that the people in the cars were reporters. They were standing beside their opened doors, resting their cameras on the car roofs. No doubt those cameras had long-range lenses –

they were probably being photographed at that very moment!

Jemima looked up at her father. She could tell that he was wrestling with the same question that was troubling her: should they cancel the trip or go to the bishop's house anyway, and arrive surrounded by a gaggle of photo-snapping reporters?

Disappointment welled up in Jemima's throat and stuck there, like a big, hard lump that would not be swallowed. She'd looked forward to this day, she had prayed for it, and now that it was here –

For the thousandth time, she wished that she had never met Brad Williams. This was his fault. But he hadn't stuck around to see the misery he'd caused -- the coward!

While they were standing there, another car crested the hill, passed the reporters, and stopped just outside their driveway. A small, wizened man poked his head out of the window.

Jemima's father had built an impenetrable and multi-layered barricade of old anvils, hay bales and rocks, and the man was obliged to get out of his car: but get out he did. When he skirted the barricade, Jacob strode down to meet him, calling:

"This is private property. You're trespassing -- get out!"

The man came ahead, and fixed his eyes on Jemima. He

called out to her: "Are you Jemima King?"

Jemima stared at him in wonder. He was a shriveled stick of a man, with a pinched, mean face: but he had courage, she had to give him that. Anyone else would be running away by now because her father had quickened his pace and was rolling up his sleeves. But she nodded slightly.

The man pulled a sheaf of rolled-up papers out of his jacket, lobbed them at her, and turned to flee. He was surprisingly nimble, but he was obliged to dash to the hay bales – and to jump over them – to avoid being caught by her angry father.

The man landed on his feet and turned at the door of his car. "Jemima King, you've been served!" Then he tried to get back into his car, but the reporters had been watching, and some of them were nimble, too. They mobbed him before he was able to get in.

Jemima was able to hear just enough to be sure that they got the whole story out of him before he slammed the car door and sped away.

Jacob stayed at the barricade and scowled at the reporters who were brave enough to linger.

"Mr. King, is your daughter being sued?"

"Who's suing Jemima, Mr. King?"

"What's she being sued for?"

Jemima was amused to see that when her mighty father made as if to climb over the barricade, even the boldest of their tormentors fled back to the safety of their cars. His Amish beliefs notwithstanding, Jacob King was not a man to be tested.

When he was satisfied that he had chased the enemy from the field, Jacob climbed the hill again. As he came, he bent down and picked up the papers that the intruder had dropped on the lawn.

Then he handed them to Jemima.

She opened them reluctantly. They were written in very formal, very legal-sounding terms, but even she could see that the papers were telling her that she was being sued.

For $1.6 million dollars.

By a man named Caldwell C. Morton.

She looked up at her father. He put an arm around her shoulder, turned her, and walked back to the house.

"Come."

They walked back inside, and Jemima could tell by the way her father looked at her, that he expected her to burst into tears. A few months ago, she would have.

But not now.

She sighed and looked up at her father's face disconsolately. "I guess I'll stay at home today, Daed," she told him, and went to seek solitude...

THANK YOU FOR READING!

I hope you enjoyed reading this sample as much as I loved writing it! If so, look for An Amish Country Treasure 3 at your favorite online booksellers.

All the Best,

Ruth

ABOUT THE AUTHOR

Ruth Price is a Pennsylvania native and devoted mother of four. After her youngest set off for college, she decided it was time to pursue her childhood dream to become a fiction writer. Drawing inspiration from her faith, her husband and love of her life Harold, and deep interest in Amish culture that stemmed from a childhood summer spent with her family on a Lancaster farm, Ruth began to pen the stories that had always jabbered away in her mind. Ruth believes that art at its best channels a higher good, and while she doesn't always reach that ideal, she hopes that her readers are entertained and inspired by her stories.